by Wanda Coleman

Mad Dog Black Lady (1979)
Imagoes (1983)
Heavy Daughter Blues (1987)
A War of Eyes and Other Stories (1988)
The Dicksboro Hotel (1989)
African Sleeping Sickness (1990)
Hand Dance (1993)

WANDA COLEMAN

HAND DANCE

BLACK SPARROW PRESS ▲ SANTA ROSA ▼ 1993

ACKNOWLEDGMENTS

Grateful acknowledgment is made to the editors of the following: *Alcatraz 2, Another Chicago Magazine, Ancient Mariners, Black American Literature Forum/African American Review, Blue Window, Caliban, City Lights Review, Cold-Drill, Colorado Review, Contact II, Cottonwood, Exquisite Corpse, Jacaranda Review, Kenyon Review, New American Writing, Obsidian II, Phoebe, Poetas De Los Angeles, Poetry/LA, Poetry New York, Post Modern Writing, Rohwedder, Santa Monica Review, Shattersheet, Urbanus, VENICE The Magazine,* and *Zyzzyva.*

Special thanks to Meri Nana-Ama Danquah and Austin Straus, who assisted in the preparation of this manuscript.

Cover photograph by Leigh Wiener.

Black Sparrow Press books are printed on acid-free paper.

LIBRARY OF CONGRESS CATALOGING-IN-PUBLICATION DATA

Coleman, Wanda.
　　Hand dance / Wanda Coleman.
　　　　p.　　　cm.
　　　ISBN 0-87685-897-3 (cloth) : $25.00. — ISBN 0-87685-898-1 (cloth signed) : $30.00.
　— ISBN 0-87685-896-5 (paper) : $13.00
　　　1. City and town life—United States—Poetry. 2. Afro-Americans—Poetry.
I. Title.
PS3553.O47447H36　　　1993
811'.54—dc20
　　　　　　　　　　　　　　　　　　　　　　　　　　　　　　　　　　　　92-45125
　　　　　　　　　　　　　　　　　　　　　　　　　　　　　　　　　　　　CIP

In memory of Ms. Uletta Jones and the
gentleness of her hands

CONTENTS

Part II: *The Sinister*

Part 4: *The laying on of . . .*

HAND DANCE

this is the ritual of the hand becoming
the whole. a body of itself
the gesture that allows
possession

> *if i am not all, who am i*
> *if i am i how am i all?*

at the tip of each finger a separate universe

> *if i am you*
> *then why aren't you me*
> *and if you are me*
> *then why the deep silence*

this is the ritual of the whole becoming the hand
shaping a certainty

to complete the cycle. to share my life
with my man. to feed my children. my hands

(they dance this anger. they sing it, paint it
make it pay. it is bigger than mere hands can hold)

> *born in slavery died enslaved*
> *yet not a slave*

> *born in misery died miserably*
> *yet not miserable*

hand story: once upon a time i laid hands in love
> *the sinister and the dexter*
> *in the hope of a man. to give him*

light by which to see me. once
upon a time i laid hands in love
to cure his flesh in the fire of
mine. burning together. once upon
a prayer

these hands

i am rooted in a tree of hands where i nest
give birth. stretch my arms to take the wind

here. a forest of hands where the only fauna
are my eyes

— Los Angeles
August 3rd, 1983

HAND DANCE

Part 1: The Dexter

ETHNOGRAPHS

1

kin to the dubbing yaw of a galleon
she shifts on her side. evokes a kick within
her belly distended by an indignant cargo
crossing uncharted atlantics
bound for troubled shores

2

made of and for toil. rooting around
in earth. stinking of sun-baked effort. a
thirst for lightning. a head rag to sop
up the grease, tuber-shaped feet sprouting eyes
arms knotty with bolls

3

well-waged the never-ending war to prove
fit humane worthy stalwart sonofason
each death for thy country a notch closer
to a cornfed glory conceived while nailed to
flustered civility and devastated hope

4

call it joy. the drum-like stomp of a foot
to bare board sets the flesh to shimmy
womanhood in loose irreverent sways against
and into the groin. call it the pull
of the great muddy

5

hands almighty dancing on skin drawn taut
the black side slidings palm-to-palm
glistenings after a hard larding down.
clammed heavenward one generation, in fists
the next. which head to comb first?

6

nothing laid claim to but what's barren
become mojo at mothering the father. strip away
the dead skin but save it to start the new
blues—an art derived from using
everything including the oink

AFRICA

ball-and-jack

a laugh so loud certain people
turn to stare

the rhythm and blues of thick lips locked tight
grinding home minutes to curfew

ass as wide as it is high

after a hard night's sex the nappy flow of
hair gone back to it

the song sung in a tub of dirty water

churchified sistuh strut with big fancy Sunday hats
workin' those stilettos

before Suez

the shadow of a shadow casting shade
on my bones

BUDDHA BELLY

the circle in the center of the hole
around which grass and mushrooms grow

the magic carpet infested with fleas
of discontent

a pillow for the head of the thinker

when seen on horizon becomes a
perfect island

the sign over the entrance to a dream

when levitated
becomes the glowing pate of the sandman

when properly rubbed brings on the ecstasy

dinner was tasty
who made noise

MISTAH MOUSE

Kika say

A refined lady-of-color was terrified of vermin. And when one took up residence in the room she rented the landlord went and got some green goop for his squeaky little ass. So he put the green goop out to bait him. And sure enuff mistah mouse showed up sniffin'. He went over to the green goop, took a bite and chew it up. And she just a watchin' damn near 'bout to faint. Li'l mistah mouse he start to scamper away when all of a sudden he got to the middle of the room and he stop. And she still watchin' to see what he gonna do. But he just stand there in mid room lookin'. So she and mistah mouse are both standing there for fifteen minutes. And she don't move and he don't move. So she say, "Don't you know you 'spose to be dead, sucka?"

So finally she go over to him and poke him. He keel over.

"And stay dead," she said.

CHAIR AFFAIR

the chair bites me. angrily i kick it

the chair wheezes every time
i sit down on it

i have decided i hate this chair
even though i need its support

the chair moves into an awkward angle every
time i get up so i am forced to look at it
before i sit down again

hard little round metallic doo-doos
keep coming out of the chair
causing me to watch my step

i have offered a truce. the loss of 25
pounds. the chair scoffs

the chair doctor states it will take
3 months and over four thousand dollars to
cure the chair

today my horoscope said avoid
recalcitrant chairs

when i came in from lunch
i found another butt in my chair

"chairs are the true plague of mankind"
— Chairman Mao

ethiopian in the fuel supplies

                    human? prove it

at school they call my son "zebra"
the black and white striping of his chromosomes
a bit darker, my daughter don't have the problem
and as the source, mama
found it made her umber-toned men uneasy

at the thought of staking claim/taking blame
for the stares of curious passersby
doin' double takes and scratchin' ass

ol' schoolmate: "saw her with them two yellow babies.
          wonder
how she caught one of *them*?"

i'm italian
i'm jew
i'm chinese

when they ask, "what are you?"

in school tired of hearing: i'm one half cajun
                            i'm one third creole
                            i'm part this part that
                            i'm neegrooo

the lighter kids laughed at me
sambolina

so i made up a story say great grandmother
was an african priestess stole from her tribe by slavers

shut evahbody up

spookanese if yah stick me hard baby
             i'll gush blood blue as the pacific on a sunny
                       day
             if yah stick me hard baby
             i'll gush blue as the pacific on a sunny day
             if yah stick me hard lover
             i'll bleed oceans for yah evah single day
             if yah stick me
             i'll drown yah and yah'll nevah get away

ghettoese   the tongue spoken in my home
             a sensual twist of english
             and black cat bone

i'm cherokee
i'm arkansas
i'm sweet molasses and do-the-do
i'm black lordy-lordy
and ogalala sioux

what are you?

say eyes
no matter how silent the mouth

(niggah in the woodpile as the sayin' goes)

"i hate it when they call me that" my son say
"i'm not a zebra—i'm me"
"human, baby"
says i, "the word is hu(e) as in color + man"

POETRY LESSON NUMBER TWO

At the party I was asked to share my work as fledgling
        ethnic poet.
It was obvious I had it somewhere on me. Anxious, I
        went into my
purse for my notebook/a concealed weapon. Blanching with
        just enough
humility I read my stuff eloquently, tossing rude epithets
        and graphic
images/pearls of street wisdom espousing Black power
        get-the-honky
and self-determination.

This gray-haired white guy approached and gave off an
        air of relaxed
well-read authority which was refreshingly lacking in
        arrogance. He
explained that he edited a small literary magazine and
        asked to
see my poems on the page.

Smugly I showed him my notebook. He read silently for a
        few minutes
as I watched him turn the pages with what I felt to be the
        proper amount
of attention deserved. I expected acceptance johnny-on-the-
        spot. Then he
dead-eyed me and said flatly, "These look *very* familiar."

Disappointed and confused by this comment, I chattily
        suggested my
poems had somehow come across his desk even though I
        had never made

the submission. They remained painfully unpublished. He shook his
head, lowered his eyes and said quietly, "Perhaps."

This conversation troubled me several weeks before the dark raised
and I finally understood his way of saying
my work lacked
originality

THE DREAM

gets up and walks
moves with grace of shadow, wind
and expresses a luminosity/urgent want
defined it is his face
above me eyes bald ejaculate white
his breath suspended and
inside me his expansion
hard to harder
we utter the thousandth name of god
i wake
the alarm clock cord at my throat
it screams/an infant
for his pacifier
knotting the noose, stealing my
air and crying to be
forgiven

MISS NATTY ANN

up central avenue thirty years gone
her mouth a room for entertaining gents
spins tales about meat market men
how dirty they are make the smell between
the thighs the funk of mold and old gold
piss and the reverb of doors swung eternally shut
on the romance of hasty knocks a visitor's
night entry she was a fancy high-yellow
dancer along dark narrow hallways tight as
"a virgin niggah gal's slit, yes Suh!"

LIKE LOVE

we're strugglin' to have meaning yet avoid
being ground into the cement by dick-head bosses and
butt-numbing jobs my ambitiousness his juvi rap sheet
smoking bush to rock and reggae we've got five bucks
        between
us and two mugs of drip grind i'm the fool-of-the-minute
slavin' overtime tryin' to turn my naught into ought
he expects that pimp success to trip over us like
a burglar over a pair of shoes our days spent as
carelessly as pennies

CHUCK MAN

that loosiana swamp dog put some funny stuff
on me. tells me i quiver his liver

he got the fish head eyes. smells like whiskey
pig feet and old smokes

he brings me okra and black-eyed peas
steady comes round to get his ham bone boiled

he do the belly rub
he do the jelly roll
he a backdoor man with front door ambition
he piss sweet water

we honky tonk we gut bucket

he scared to leave his wife she a two-headed
woman. the fix go deep

he feed me catfish promises
he feed me divorce lies

he ain't strong enuff to leave her
i ain't strong enuff to make him stay

on odd mornings he come round early
try to catch another niggah in my bed

to work his mojo he lick my pearl to
feel it glow. makes my hair grow

BLUES FOR THE MAN ON SAX (2)

wind whispers

longsleep pooped out at the party, double duty got
no time to kill. some jig stole the fifty out of her bra.
and she didn't even get a kiss. mascaraed misery trying
to make it on her own tappin' the till

wind sighs

she ran butt-pumping brandishing the machete after the
landlady who told her to get her ass out. she cried for
three hours on Mama Creole's porch 'bout her man in
Korea/a professional soldier had to get away from
all that smothering mambo

wind tears

scalded with boiling water he fled his skin/their bed
screaming. and she watched ever so calmly having upped
the ante on two-timing. later he would forgive her. later
she would take up stargazing

wind yowls

the collector paused blood running from her elbows
dripping down the portrait. o temptation. where the shot
came from, a mystery. it pierced the clock and made
night a permanent thing

DR. MUNGO

poet to poet a rage score

caught between chiliast & nirvana

today i heard your haunted echo enticing me
beyond the confines of this cement cubicle
slicing thru my frantic reordering of
assigned madnesses hoping i won't be fingered
scheming an evasion

your name came sudden to sear my eyes
jumped up at me from the page a line running boldly
thru it

have you gone to join tanabe on his sojourn
to Tibet? are you afloat in the cosmic
garbage of homeless indigents? are you on hold
in the barred penal tanks of Christ-like
solitude? is your mythic presence entombed in
cryptic spoons of skagg or blow?

or do you do sweet lady who has ultimately done you?

you crossed my mind today, Doc Mungo. i
heard the hasty shuffle of your stagger
and am returning the call

WE MEET THE BLACK RIMBAUD

as we exit the elevator we step into the
Santa Cruz of 1981. the dark inebriated hallways of
Hotel St. George call my name and ask who allowed
me in. we sense a sudden spasm in our direction.
it is he. he lurches outside our lovers' suite.
he stumbles besotted besnotted
in purples blues and browns—he of the deeply
cratered psyche toast-colored skin and lunar eclipses
half-Negro half-Jew all reeking devastation
(having spent ten years in a notsolongago lifted
self-proclaimed silence) having that afternoon been
booed off and having been carried from the stage
in the tender adoration of saxophone and
double bass. he spies us recognizes us and invites us
to the party in the court of the king of beatitude
(Harry Silver and the gang are there)
where coverts rasp eloquently on the exasperations
of those sobered by the enthused applause of failed
versifiers and a doggerel pursuit that nets only
the promise of a hamilton and a rubber check.
as we watch, the legend staggers wall-to-wall
sloshings from his glass splash to the hungry floor
and are quickly drunk. and while we know who he is
we are reintroduced as fellow spooks to this specter
dancing on marbles. and when he hears his name he
looks askance shudders hisses and asks

"Bob Kaufman? *Who* is Bob Kaufman?"

ODE FOR DONNY HATHAWAY

and then there are the one-hit zombies
cursed to an eternity of Monday nights

who runs our music does not make it
controls manufacture and marketing of rhythm
schemes on and fixes the charts. it's polyphonic greed
from the dark of the chitlin to solid gold dawn
doublecrossed over

a love come down

after the plunge
sloshing around in limbo

that too sweet gospel splash

GEORGE 1990

he got nearer and nearer

till all he needed was the mere corner of the room

a chair in front of the television set
or at the side of the dining table

to nod hours at a time

washing dishes constituted a day's work
along with emptying the trash and poring
over dusty things in the garage

watering the lawn

his edentulous conversations limited to
coughs gasps sighs laughs grunts a tsk-tsk
head tilted slightly right or left
shoulders hunched

the bathroom a war zone

he kept his fobless watch loose in a pocket
he kept his wallet stuffed with snapshots
and business cards. he kept his boxer's grip

glasses always misplaced
sweaters worn regardless of climate or time of day

the nearer he got the more self-contained

for the girl with cerebral palsy

you dive into a spasm and twist your sweetness
as we bend toward you to understand
words thick-tongued and fresh with spittle
your body rocking your eyes rolling with self-impatience
your arms angling against air

you've come to the decision to give up
your child. afraid you will go off, leave him
and he will starve. yes you love him but cannot
love yourself the mirror image of parents
unable to "love imperfection"

and now you unfold before us the origami of your
shame. a ring of strange paper dolls holding ragged
hands/jagged pieces of tissue too frail
even for tears

DESERT MOTHER

under lava mud ash
glimmer salt flats a parched and monotonous shimmer
in fierce sun a blaze of delicate-hued vegetation
tamarind & pepper, date palms & sycamore
cottonwoods & willows
the floodplain of sand surrounded by low peaks
sepia lavender gray unrelieved desolation
bleached rolling foothills
black precipices
occasional clusters of adobe and stucco
yields of gold borax turquoise moonstone agate
phantasmagoria. the plunge westward
sparse rainfall and torrid midnights
joshua fit to battle
her crater runs deep a volcano
once thought extinct

HERITAGE

the Dakota man came to the party
among strangers—mainly whites
at our table my husband told him that i, his wife
was part Sioux (a breed indian)
embarrassed that he would tell this story to
an *authentic* of tribal origin
i was nevertheless polite and did not deny my history
otherwise there wasn't much we had in common
for me the afro-american dominated the aboriginal
and i had no further evidence with which
to state my case until, reaching for a butter knife
i noticed his hand. look, i said, and held my hand
next to his. except for color
they were the same

FEBRUARY 11TH 1990

—for Dennis Brutus

This year the leaves turn red green black
freedom colors each leaf
each stitch of grass. I am amazed
at my sweet harvest. The prison door has opened
and a nation's heart is released. I am full
having spent my greediness in a ritual of joy.

BUTTAH

endless wobbles

when seen rear-view we sistuhs
who got the cadillac walk
frequently stop traffic
my gift from my mother sits awkwardly
on father's frame

weights me down when i walk
quick steps take maximum effort
throw off my center of gravity
running the definitive chore

many have experienced this
ultimate wiggle/have happily disappeared
into like convolutions of
hot american rum and bitter-sweet
african rhythm

many

and many have been reborn of it

BLUE GLASS

my thighs open, release his face

the luscious tint of the nouveau art deco lamp in the store
window an artifact of cold glistening midnight the scratchy
whine of a gramophone the seductive caress of a steamy
room when the radiator starts to sing. my pulse rushes
i ache to put my cheek against it/into it, lick the past
of down-home brown bawdy house floozies knotting garters
behind moth-eaten velveteen high on boo and big talk

my smile fits his face like an arm-length satin glove

love-world evoked in the mirrored surface of mama's coffee
table an exact replica of the original pane. i live under
the reflection, sneak a drunk off the waft of fresh-cut irises,
Chanel No. 5 and *Lullaby of Birdland*. she's the fancy dame
in fox fur pelts over houndstooth tailored suit with padded
shoulders—he's the conk-haired dap daddy in pinstripe zoot
smelling of musk oil and excess

my scream shattering his face

intravenous video/eyes old channels a constant yen for
ancient laugh tracks and reruns of bride of the
zombie. his distaste for sunlight misinterpreted as
elemental cool school jazzy coveting of born-again cathode.
in black & white i safari lost continents of love,
programmed for the murder-suicide of the boom generation,
my second heart on remote control. meanwhile the late night
cartoon enters a sanitarium to kick his viewing habit

what i see the world thru

JUMP SONG

put on your white bone sneakers
and your two-tone peepers
meet the train at the station
we gonna go to washington
and cause a sensation

tell mister president tell congress too
gonna agitate to legislate and do the do

put on your white bone sneakers
and your two-tone peepers
buy yourself a ticket
meet the train at the station
we going to the promised land
and cause a sensation

when you get to the junction
flag the special down and tell
the conductor to take it underground

when he hits the breaker
it'll be a bone shaker
so put your teeth back in before
you meet your maker

SEX AND POLITICS IN FAIRYLAND

rose red from across the tracks does
grow up to be a knockout. bold with big legs
and all the rest of the equipment necessary
to excite a prince

and if she plays her pumpkins right (she will)
she'll become snow white will acquire
all the material things wished upon

the big fine castle. servants of a darker race
the stretch limo. jewels and furs
champagne for a frivolous breakfast of
scrambled eggs and caviar

a smart dame from across the tracks, rose
has an instinct for opportunity—the savvy it
takes to get over. she knows she's got to score
before she's knocked up, starts to pudge out, or
otherwise loses her looks

this may require compromise—dyeing her hair
henna or ash, special hormones or cosmetic surgeries
and pretending a certain amount of ignorance
about the workings of fairytales

there will be critical moments when one word from
rose would change the story's plot. but she knows
her role and will hold her tongue. history
is the thorny realm of rich powerful princes

in the meantime rose can play games with trolls and
witches. her prince will tolerate it as long as

she doesn't cross him. as long as her game
doesn't interfere with his

and if she wants she can even make a sport of
equal height between normals & dwarfs. he will
understand. she needs to do something for
amusement — as long as the dwarfs
remain dwarfs

he will even allow her a wolf or two

thus our gal rose needn't concern herself
with the eternal sleep threatening the kingdom
she is assured resurrection by the local
sorcerer who offers happy endings
at a discount

JUICE MONEY

looking for meaning i motor in circles towards
downtown in a smog south now east now north
back west along a gray narrowness making a right at
the second light. something red screams stop
i ease the brakes to a squeak. intracellular pressure
i can't see the sun. it's overcast and cool

pulling into a fast-stop-quick-shop i spy this gangster
in ragged denims his right lower leg in a plaster cast
protected by a neatly wrapped trash bag he's into
heavy loiter hustles a gray boy for change after
slap-dashing his windshield. he sees me seeing him

"hey Sugaroo, iszat yo' cahr?" he smiles as i pass
"yeah, what's left of it" i sing over my shoulder
my tore-down Buick evokes his soft laughter
he sees we're coming from the same place

but the store don't carry the proof of stress relief
required to take my mind off — to liberate my erythrocytes.
if only i had the peace
or the mind

hastily he sincerely takes his brown terry rag and
busts the escapees from the ozone layer. i check him
out. five years ago we might've done more than chuckle
like conspirators — ebony skins good looks
hungry white teeth

at whose service?

what's left to enjoy under the guise of what?
game after game for pretense of acceptance
bone on bone

i'm reminded of Manhattan bloods hostile in their
assault on denizen drivers, forcing them to pay
spraying like whacked-out captain zodiacs
spraying for juice money/enuff to score
spraying foam thick as cum

i decline his offer to wash my rear window
he smiles again insisting he finish the job/a good
worker/would-be lover if-and-when
i go into my wine kidskin wallet for a neatly
furled Washington
"thanx, Sugaroo. be good now," he laughs again
tucks it away

i fire the ignition and resume pursuit of my
own tail. what's left of morning settles
around my eyes a darkly visible weight

and they say good black don't crack

still arguing God

LOVIN' BREAKFAST BLUES

i want cream in my coffee, baby
and sugar in my tea
i like cream in my coffee
and sweet sweet sugar in my tea
got to have that love rush, baby
to keep my energy

i want butter on my muffin, lover
and jam on my hot toast
i need butter on my muffin
and jelly on my hot brown toast
but molasses on my biscuits
is the thrill i love the most

turn my eggs over easy, honey
and fry my bacon crisp
turn my eggs over easy easy
and fry my bacon crisp
put some onions in my hash browns
and a banana in my dish

refrain: give me lovin' in the morning
give me lovin' all day thru
let me keep on steady greasin'
cuz i've so much love for you
feed me in between meals
or give me chicken on the run
just remember darlin'
a good love's never done

cream in my coffee, lover
and sugar sugar in my tea
i need some o' dat cream in my coffee

and sugar in my tea
when i stir it up and drink it
it tastes so doggone good to me

THE ECONOMICS OF SKIN

feeling-based ritual is shunned as is
social parity and fair pay

mine a house of shame in a hood
where emigré neighbors prosper yet regard
me with fear/noses open as my queen-size
darkness evokes mystery and a
compulsion to finger-pop

from my brief whiff of the top-ten university
i learned it is rude to discuss money in
mixed company. rudely i discuss it
the red and the black of it
my lack and what that lack wreaks
(we pea-brains believe in the merits of
old-fashioned honest hard work/get your hands
dirty/that man or woman is only as good
as his/her word)

nuthin' could be finah than
a breakfront fullah china

inside this poor person is a rich one
struggling to get out

THE ASHMAN

over green felt i side-pocket the 8-ball
but scratch/fear cushioned in bravado
a little english to quiet the loins

when genuine laughter requires practice

beneath the flaking concrete sky
i'm made privy to the subversion the satchel
brimming with wills as he educates me on how to
promo grief sufficient to inspire suicide

pipe dream or pipe bomb

the lust assassin specializes in
financially well-endowed widows and divorcees
lingers long enough to liquefy assets and
collect the insurance check

frequents crematoriums

can his cultural-nationalist sexual revolutionary
plot to hold affection ransom succeed?

to live for is to cry for
strung out on girl and snot

nuthin' in my heart but trust
nuthin' in my purse but dust

DREAM 1812

nude in bed
i raise my left thigh to pick at a troubling
blackhead on the lower inner aspect. it looks unusual
and sits at the center of a perfect aureole/deeper brown
against my cocoa skin

"shit," i think, "i hope this isn't cancer"

i put my thumbs together and squeeze, nothing happens so
i squeeze harder. the blackness starts to emerge. suddenly an
egg-sized mass pops up, a nipple and the aureole crown it. i'm
astonished by the tiny breast which jiggles in morning light

as i get up to see how it'll feel to walk, i notice a 4-inch
cylindrical umber growth has emerged from my left leg just
below my knee. it's narrow at the base and extremely rigid.
frightened i reach to pull it off and white stuff like liquid
taffy shoots from its head, gets all over the bed, the floor, my
hands then the thing goes flaccid. i'm cleaning up the mess
with a towel when my lover appears

"look," i say, "new appendages"

he examines the inside of my thigh as i speculate on this
being a twin submerged in me since birth. i show
him the penis and his eyes light up

"hmmmmm," he says, "the next time it gets hard, call me"

MY SHOW

—for Charlene Wolfe

to watch requires being home religiously
at that certain air time
my favorite munch my favorite drink
hot or cold
obligations on ice, phone off the hook

i kick back in the broken bed the grungy lounge
chair or unfold against the lumpy sofa or
slide into the rusty tub for a long soak
and video

there to observe as the manikins of Make Believe
strut thru fantasies i might've concocted
with all the glamour gadgets beyond my
fiduciary pale

to escape the mirror/my unable self
in pursuit of unobtainables
my futile pink-collar drone
devoid of fun

(the confessions of a part-time ebony couch spud)

tv therapy is as cheap as it comes
besides
some trash is good trash

HE TAKES HER TO THE MOVIES

at the walk-in concession counter his
arms surround and embrace. she jumps
unaccustomed to public displays of tenderness
it takes a moment to unwind
into his fold

he prefers chocolate to popcorn
she reminisces about drive-ins

revivals turn him on as do existential
european visions or comedies with
cultural references to the Catskills
or Brooklyn. she's keen on film noir of
the 40s and 50s — anything to escape
her umber skin for an hour or two

she remembers when they cost fifty cents
he remembers when they cost a nickel

sometimes one asks the other
"did i see that with you?"

in the theatre's dark she is
now and then startled by slight muffled
sniffles mid-scene. the glow from
the silver screen illuminates
his tears

after the movies
they hold hands

FALSE SPRING

an uncanny raucous chirp chirp is heard
as mockful birds suddenly appear making nests
quarrelsome with unexpected matings
and the heady blush of bugs 'n such stir 'n sting anew
enthralled lovers stroll neath a startled blue sky
hayfever aroused prematurely by the lusty santanas
blinds me with sneeze
and my restless lay moves on to moister ground
(and they say i've never known snow)
it is the middle of winter California-style
tell that to the magenta butterflies
blossoms pink and yellow limbs bared scanty weeks ago
even the trees are deceived

SMALL TALK ABOUT THE WEATHER

mama, what is clouds?

theys the souls of people who died
and didn't want to go to heaven cuz they love
this earth so much

what's rain then?

that's they tears when they sad
to see all the bad things happenin' down here

and when it thunders and storms
and makes lightning?

theys real mad then. theys
real mad

BRIEF VISIT TO PARADISE

no. he is not responsible for this fix
      i'm in even if he
is one of them and i've come to him as
      seraphic benefactor
one sympathetic to my cause if not direct
      supporter of it
i have come to him for help to his grand house
      where he lives in
great comfort with his angelic family i have
      come so angry
about the necessity to maintain shelter this
      urgency this
emergency born of my incurable skin condition
      i have come to
request a loan which i will pay back somehow
      someday if in
blood as i fight back outraged tears my eyes my
      heart straining
under great embarrassment i swallow my pride
      mountains of it
humble myself that i may feed my children
      another week or
two until i can make my own luck my own way
      find a piece of money
steal it if need be this melodrama my cursed
      planetary survival
my gnat's ass as precious as congolese gold
      my flyspeck of
existence as majestic as mississippi sunrise
      i sit and wait for
him in his garden so full of shame i think the
      roses are watching

as minutes crawl and creep until finally he
        returns to hand
me a palmful of alms. "all i can afford"
        says the grand man
in his grand eden surrounding his grand house
        and i accept his
words as gospel graciously swallowing my rage
        i give my bitter
thanks and promise the pay-back. as i leave my
        spirit shrunken
so small i trip over an ant and suddenly the
        sky is filled
with the uproarious laughter of roses

SHIT WORKER IN GENERAL

i do good things for the good dead

i type up their manuscripts
   dust off their mementos
   polish their brass spittoons
i march in the parades celebrating
   their having been
i watch them on old film footage
   speak to them in the dark
   light candles if asked (altho they understand
   they do have to ask)
i gather up their dirty laundry
   sweep up after them (but i refuse to feed
   their cats)

i keep the minutes of their meetings
   and collect the dues

THE TAO OF UNEMPLOYMENT

things wait until funds are insufficient
then deconstruct in concert

the aura of fear offends management
cultivate false confidence. to pretend one
does not need is to muzzle resistance

in the fractured mirror of public intercourse
care for self beneath all distortions
wisdom is an old wardrobe kept in good repair

hunger is most attractive when gaunt
generosity when opulent. practice the craft of
lean-staying. a skinny soul makes a fat tongue

the profits of love increase
with credit validation

learn to tolerate what one must demean oneself
to do in order to meet one's obligations

false smile false laugh feigned enthusiasm
sublimate resentments and overlook affronts
to appear natural is mastery
the quiet hand collects

spirit health springs from the reservoir
of self-respect. never forget
who is being fooled

TALK ABOUT THE MONEY

i need to talk hard cash. how to make it work
how to not be afraid of it. how to make it user friendly
how to plant it and make it sprout or tame
it cage it and admire its ferocious beauty
(all the more beautiful for being in my capture)
how to satisfy it and in return, have it satisfy

i need to talk serious money. how it fuels passion
how it endows with power. how and what insufficient
quantities of it aborts. we need to talk money. to
understand the current currency of our time. what it
means to survive in this new dawn of the whore

we cannot afford to be naive. ignorance and being
sincere solve nothing. we need to speak coin
to establish credit. to lift ourselves
by our own purse-straps

we need to be able to bank on each other

to live life in the black

DREAM 516

witchin' hour ensues as i cruise a blues neighborhood
in my tore down coupe. it's just the kind of spot i'm
spooking for. i'm not sure what i want only i crave it
it's a dark south central southwest corner, a two-story
apartment complex with tall sliding glass paneled
windows and gold numbers on teak-colored pine. in
cool-fool fashion i lean into my horn, make two quick honks,
the first muffled, the second sharp, clear. i climb out
to see who happens

the air smells of ham hocks and greens. one-by-one all doors
ease open. in each stands a heavyset Black man silhouetted
against gold-lit interiors, each a specter who waits to hear
his name. as i grope to find my tongue, one man in his 50s
steps thru glass and smiles. his face is a semisweet chocolate
mask of hustle and jive, a prominent nose and glossy black
conked hair. he wears beige slacks and a polished cotton
short-sleeved shirt open 3 buttons down. a gold medallion
mounts his chest

"who do you want?" he asks
"i don't know."
"what do you want to score?"
"i'm not sure."
"we deal in anything anytime. but you must be specific."

he turns and waves, a signal as those other-worldly *bruthas*
back away one-by-one and close their doors

confused, i thank him, say maybe i'll return when all
comes clear. he nods and walks me to my car.

i wake to find i've left the lights on all night and
am clutching the complete works of
William Shakespeare

ANALECTS

in the world of game best game
no game at all

bettah ugly girl stay ugly than
have illusion of cosmetic beauty fail

when black man fuck it's political

handwriting on the wall
is usually that of gang member

old man can buy you car
but bettah mileage with younger man

black is beautiful white is beautiful
but black stays beautiful longer

eating shit is principal occupation
of one who lacks courage

the man who talks a lot in bed
talks a lot out of bed

black man successful in business
will be given the business

vigorous woman have more fun teaching
young lover new tricks than getting
old lover to remember his

money will see young couple thru
time of no love bettah than love
will see them thru time of no money

the way to a black man's heart
is thru white man's wallet

2 kind of criminal: those by choice
those with no voice. 2 kind of
crime: possession and passion

only 3 kind of man need woman's money
unemployed disabled and dead

only dog receives
equality from dog

the street of dreams
is a crowded avenue

APTITUDE TEST

three black men standing on the corner are

a) a riot
b) a street gang
c) winos
d) a do-wop trio
e) all of the above

three black women standing on the corner are

a) Jehovah's Witnesses
b) whores
c) angry mothers chasing down errant sons
d) on their way to a bake sale
e) fighting over a man

a white man driving thru a black neighborhood is

a) a child molester
b) an undercover cop
c) a government agent
d) a truant officer
e) a john

a white woman seen in a black neighborhood is

a) a prostitute
b) poor white trash
c) a social worker
d) an undercover cop
e) a mental hospital escapee

a white couple driving thru a black neighborhood

a) took the wrong freeway exit
b) are delivering turkey dinners on Thanksgiving
c) are on their way to open up the shop
d) are visiting their mulatto grandchild
e) are missionaries

a black man walking thru a white neighborhood is

a) a burglar
b) a gardener or factotum or chauffeur
c) making a delivery
d) bourgeois
e) on his way to score

a black woman walking thru a white neighborhood is

a) a domestic
b) a kept woman
c) making a delivery
d) bourgeois
e) a door-to-door cosmetic sales lady

a black couple driving thru a white neighborhood

a) are entertainers
b) are going to the boss's dinner party
c) are visiting their mulatto grandchild
d) are house hunting
e) took the wrong freeway exit

a foreigner walking thru a black neighborhood is

a) a bag man for a drug cartel
b) a liquor store owner
c) a chicken franchise owner
d) a real estate agent
e) the new neighbor from a war-torn country

She was flattered to be invited to perform on campus. There were several big names on program. She hoped for enough spill-over to give her a little bit of a crowd. When she got to the room where she was to give her recital, there was no audience. The event was to start in fifteen minutes. People began to straggle in at five minutes to the hour. Gratefully, she counted twelve rather lethargic listeners. The woman who was to introduce her was late, and so at ten minutes after the hour she rose and introduced herself. She groaned inwardly. The acoustics were very raspy as they tended to be in classrooms. There was no microphone. She would have to project. As she was about to start, an old Hasid entered the room. He looked out-of-place and she wondered why he had come; surely, not to hear her? And so she went into her *thang* quite intensely, expecting half of the audience to walk out — particularly the old man who had lodged himself against a wall in the back. When he showed no sign of budging, she relaxed and got into her groove. She finished to enthusiastic applause and smiles on the faces of her listeners — all but the Hasid. As she gave out autographs and accepted warm hugs, he watched mutely as if bearing witness. She collected her honorarium from the embarrassed hostess who had tiptoed into the room after everything was over. As she said goodbye to her last convert the Hasid rose from his seat and approached her. She turned to him, curious. "Yes?" He owl-eyed her. "As I sat and listened to you, I tried to decide what kind of woman you are." He shook an ancient forefinger at her. "And then I looked at that and that and that." He pointed at her bracelets of copper and silver and the rings — she wore one or two on each finger of both hands. "And I *know* what kind of woman you are." He about-faced and indignantly stomped off. She stood wondering, briefly stung. She had absolutely no idea what he had meant and dismissed it as something cultural.

HOLLYWOOD THEOLOGY

feathers-in-our-head men
pow-wow

the lions didn't eat enuff christians
to save me from the emasculation
of my people tongue/drum

mohammed has no use for bodacious black clits
(the 7th heaven a nooky nada)

the trappings of buddha's hybrid cult offspring
give me moonshine fits

atheistic apropos-grams have failed to explain
holistic apparitions appearing nightly
on sunset & vine

and talmudic cloakings in the torrid temple
have taught me kabbalistic curiosities
(red rules)

tao bahai saknoti nikto

i ching all over
s.w.a.t. angst

sri sir — so sri. i'm barefoot in the vermudi

which witch?

they say the followers of doctor john
jumped the jive of jim jones (aka baius)

still walk the jungle night
de zombie who do do

on second thought, i'll follow mister chan
it's safer

REFUGEE FROM VACAVILLE

isolation
therapy/strapped down on the cement slab
cold-cocked for days in that empty lair
is how he got those eyes—moist and pleading

in the space for race on his birth certificate
his mother lied, put "white" thinking
it'd make life easier vis-à-vis pwt
his olive cast brought on suspicion whenever he tried
        to pass
on his rap sheet he is known
for the nigger he is

in reform school a dark buddy covered his ass
protected him from being beat up for not being black enuff
but was later knifed by some rich white boy
whose father pulled string

juvenile antics do not become adults
he didn't know how to be big time—joy ride
rob and do dope—until a count of grand theft auto
got him three hots and the proverbial cot

o the prison stripe—it put the hurt on
                it put the big vein
                it put the lullaby
                it put the light on

in the penitentiary the homosexual haunchos
think him too ugly to molest
on the streets
he picks women willing to warden

COLORISM

he and i sat by poolside
he, many shades brighter than i

enviously we spied on the visitors from Senegal
as they dove and splashed about in the pool
with flawless pure black silk for skin

"goddamn," said i, "look at them. they make
me feel contaminated"

"humph!" he snorted. "how do
you think i feel?"

DÉJÀ FAIT

he sleeps in the exact same spot he slept in
the exact same bed arms around me in the exact same
way and likes like him to lay up on Sunday mornings
has the same size feet likewise hazel eyes his birth
month, his long brown wavy hair (ditto) the
shower running and he also preferred showers his clothes
i keep watching his clothes to see if they, too, will
disappear

mouth echoing bitch

ESSAY ON LANGUAGE (2)

before slavery

my people-tongue (drum) was sure. there were no excesses. those who spoke it knew the work of tribal time during which they were not native but simply a history apart in which the cycles of life played out in accordance to the rhythms of that other continent

oh we all speak

eloquently of the introduction of the Atlantic into our speech. the middle passage. remember those who dove from the dutch ship into the deep, sacrificing themselves and their children, who cheated slavery in death. it was at this time a spiritual rending and longing (holler) was introduced into our tongue

so that even now

there are those still throwing themselves into the sea so-to-speak

landed and chained

our metaphor was denied, was first made "sin" against the mores of a slaving race, then "crime." the english tongue was enforced/ whipped into our flesh enough to make our servitude profitable. with the denial of our tongue, our creeds and worships were also denied. (in english our men and women have become genderless/interchangeable as "nigger") thus a new sorrow was born and it too entered our tongue and created a resonance (blues) which distinguishes ours from all european speech and sets us apart even from those with whom we urge reunion and so we found

thru deceit, ways to keep our tongue alive. to let it live within us though departed from our source. to become the tongue itself (attitude) so that it speaks even in our bodily movements. so that it seduces english, snaking back to ourselves. so that the dominant tongue, once infected with our hunger will one day succumb without divining what has happened (unspoken)

and even now i

gibber in my diverse postures, cajoling and conjuring. this spelling out. this gospel. it is about being and recognition of being. my tongue alive in my particular vocalizations, chorusing with like others also singing

it be about bones doin' somethang

WHAT IT MEANS TO BE DARK

when you are beaten
it is more difficult for scars to be seen

in all chase scenes
you are the bad guy. chaser or chasee

when shot it is more difficult to see
bullet holes therefore easier for them
to keep shooting

of course you're always hostile

of course you're always paranoid and overly
sensitive about your race

of course you fail to appreciate that some of them
have tough lives too

are you your brutha's keeper?
even though he sold you out

— darkness quiz —

no one asks if: a) you are a virgin
　　　　　　　　b) you've ever been to jail
　　　　　　　　c) you drink alcohol or use dope
　　　　　　　　d) you are a thief
　　　　　　　　e) you can dance good
　　　　　　　　f) all of the above

you know you are in the dark when they sit
you at the table nearest the kitchen
and you take immediate umbrage even if
it's the only table available and
is offered out of expediency

to the other Wanda Coleman
— with apologies

the phone rings again. something clicks. it's dangerous
to touch that thing
day or night

the sudden heaviness of breath/a hiss/a piercing
"bitch"

his voice gone, leaves a terrible resonant
anger

she shudders. why all this? why me? what have i
done? this is the shits
why don't they get us straight? i'm me
and she's she

she writes i write she's black i'm black
but other than that
we're nothin' the like

and while in the same place at just about
the same time — we've never met

dreaded moment: my name called from the podium
we both stand

double bubble gum

dear world,
we know who's who. when will you? she's had hers
disconnected

GIRLFRIENDS

—for Mungen, Rosen & Feldman

we are faced with the irrefutable analyses
no one's gonna pay us for what's left of
our gal youth and our lady beauty

a connection in New York, London or the Vatican
is worth the expense of self-transmission as in
send bio demo-tape shoe size and lock of hair

there the need to be heard there the need there
are no proper men to fill there the nights so empty
we occupy ourselves with compulsive telephoning
and radio talk shows

forty smackers per diem and the secretarial pool
are alternatives to etching our names into toilet
stall walls with bobby pins (we shit, therefore)

we look after our mothers as we would have
our children look after us

we know the rhythms of loss and cancer intimately

we are constantly in the mirror of each other's
hope for "get over," networking against the next
wrinkle and unemployment check

we are the soft-armed stubborn avant garde
of the new cornucopia knowing we will be too
snaggle-toothed for the feast
once it arrives

we stroke each weary other to heal for this is
not about mutual masturbation but familial
respect and unmitigated pride. creativity is
the color of our skins

we write therefore we are

DICKSBORO REFLECTIONS

the glass spider spins passion's web
across the full-length mirror. his ghostly
prints dance in dust along the edges of
overstuffed bookcases

her blue bruised palms his urgent sweat

screenless windows painted shut
the lemon-orange glare of afternoon sun
against gray shades in hot smogless november
the musk of wet rug freshly bleached of oil paint
and blood

bridging the distance of skin

the jittery tock-tock of a white plastic clock
squat atop the aged video console
dull buzz of a solitary fly
a roach of bo in the seldom used ashtray

when loneliness inspires entertainment

the unmade dilapidated murphy bed broken
under pressure sheets dirty the ill-patched
mattress and quilt sprawled to the floor
the turning suddenly into each other

her soiled stretch-alls his dirty jocks
wine glasses emptied of woe
the crumpled untyped anniversary poem
silence sighs silence again followed by
whispers followed by sighs

not what you do, who

AMERICAN SONNET (3)

fair splay/pay—the stuff myths are made of
(cum grano salis)

that thoughts become things
words weapons

who gives the african violet the right to bloom
rain the right to be wet
who permits the moon to draw menses

i protest this tyranny of ghosts
who reign in the world of letters
would-be-betters

in actuality

pseudo-intellectuals with suck-holes for brains
so dense even when the light goes on
they're still in the dark

today i protest the color of the sky
that is not the color of my skin

Part 2: The Sinister

THE HEEBEEGEEBEES

are transmitted by closets

can be gotten from sniffing the insides of
old soles or from heavy doses of
talk-show television

can be contracted while staring at pink ovals
of soap during bathtub soaks

come on after jive converse over
gas station pay phones in early AMs
or episodes of clutching the steering wheel
too tightly

live for 48-hours on the rims of dreams

he took his lover in parts

hid her stark white teeth in the sugar canister. he
laid her ears gently between the pages of a gigantic tome,
pressed it shut, returned it to the library shelf. her nose,
hands and feet are buried outside in back under the
lavender rose bush. her legs, arms and torso were
cast into the pacific after midnight. all internal organs
were ground up and fed to the cats. her skull was drained,
crushed, ground into fine powder and sold as
aphrodisiac. he got her all

except those elusive eyes

JERRY 1965

being with him is being accepted/his wife
they live on a diet of soaps, horror movies and
trashy novels. she is grossly pregnant and
always hungry. he tries hard to figure it out. she's
a true believer, so proud of her cracker jack
rhinestone ring she's about to bust

the movement that brought him west is dying
there's nothing in this city he can make money at
art a better excuse for poverty than ignorance
she spends her hours daydreaming over lime sodas
cracking "polly seeds" for the salt

he stagnates when not showing off to a crowd
strumming that bum twelve-string (when out of hock)
wailing about wildwood flowers and trains bound
for glory between drags on that tone deaf harmonica

when hope went sex followed

CONFESSIONS NOIRES

i am afraid of telephones

one of my greatest highs is city driving
before sunrise after rain, listening

frequently the likeness of my first husband
masks the faces of our children calling to mind
an inscription i made on a photo—some hogshit
about his being my first my last

i hate dresses

i have no fear of needles
only users of needles

the only thang i'm hooked on these days
is money. withdrawal pangs are constant

i'm not the type, said i
all women are the type said he
and if you're not it's going to be quite a
pleasure finding out what type you are

my worst nightmares are about telephones

once i pulled off a robbery
got away with the goods, then, like a fool
gave them to my lover-of-the-moment
to impress him

Ann Petry wrote my life's story published the year
i was born

90

i prefer commercials over programming
black and white over color
informed silence over ignorant applause

i pray only on airplanes

occasionally one of my dreams
comes true

once in a while i pass myself going
in the other direction

i am afraid of the light
at the end of a poem

436 MOONS

my graying kinks
my heteromorphic tongue my jealous claws
my feet stones set in leather

along my legs sinew snaps and
spasms (the willies)

travel this white path of fear

will i be another thrill-kill
another statistic consigned to bureaucratic doom

i've taken up residence on the edge
and can't make this month's rent

"genius is a liability to you," said the gypsy
"play dumb"

free in my nothing my no time

in the world i come from
violence is a language and a bullet
sudden insight

AMERICAN SONNET (4)

rejection can kill you

it can force you to park outside neon-lit
liquor stores and finger the steel of
your contemplation. it can even make you
rob yourself

(when does the veteran of one war fail to
appreciate the vet of another?)

the ragged scarecrow lusts in the midst of
a fallow field

and the lover who prances in circles envies me
my moves/has designs on my gizzard/kicks shit

this is the city we've come to
all the lights are red all the poets are dead
and there are no norths

CROAKERS

on harlem avenue on gladys they're drunk off
derision and the aroma of unwashed bodies
unkempt clothes and uncollected garbage
by midnight hundreds of stumblers are blindly
eclipsed by something tantamount to death as
they crouch by fires of blazing waste
tonight a thin blue hope's about to snap/life's
pull this gloom of heading nowhere lucky to
be unmolested by the cops or tougher scavengers
clawing crawling these gilt gutters a gang of
analyses doomed to statistical disappearances
skidding into the crack of no return

THE THIEF OF SPADES

i wake him angry at 6 a.m. i scream, "why'd you
steal the kid's money? what'd you do with it?"
he denies it. comes all the way woke. i
tremble with anger tell him he's
got to get out. we can't live like this
can't breathe in this ugly
and there's nothing in his face
nothing to nail my hope on
and he says for the umpteenth time
"i didn't take it"
"don't tell me that shit don't tell me
that shit" i repeat and salivate, my fists
clenched i take a step toward him. "i'm this far
from jumpin' into your ass" i threaten
and he takes a step back. the stirrings of
the kids interrupt and it's a gruesome truce over
coffee. i know it's only a matter of days
before he's gone for good

WHAT THE MOON SAW

not a wolf but a slew of jackals. the ax dropped by the
terrified woodsman who fled in thwarted heroism. the
basket overturned—a feast spilled and left to things
that crawl. a shattered wine bottle its vintage gushing silver
rivulets in the grass. shreds/a red flannel cape and hood. the
sanguine-stained tatters of pink gingham. the glints off an
army of teeth at work on the flesh of a luscious fresh kill

HIS COMMENTS AFTER HER HANGING

a few days after the workshop
we found her suspended from a noose
remarkably she'd made it herself out of rope
i didn't know she felt that way

she was a good person, really
i used to see her around
we'd talk, you know, and sometimes
she'd come down to the workshop and listen

she had a cat. she talked to it
i don't know what's happened to it
it showed up here once. i fed it
and then it disappeared

if only she'd spoken up.
to anyone

it's such a waste. hanging

and you know, she wasn't a bad looking woman
not at all

AKBAR THE MAD POET

otherwise known as someone else, take luther
alphonse rivers or david ravon smith

half black half white. a brown eye on his left
his right eye blue

he regurgitates anguish as brutality
what is in his gut goes to his head

on one occasion Akbar is spotted in downtown
Manhattan slamming the head of his lover thru
a plate glass window. this earns him straightjacket
time and diagnosis as schizophrenic

(ain't dat da natch'l order o Niggah Universe?
all Blacks are schizo. African vs. American
we just can't get along with ourselves)

after that episode
he abandons the apple for the orange

one sunny afternoon Akbar is found wandering nude
along the stretch of Venice Beach his face bloody
his blue eye freshly plucked from its socket
the offender crushed
in his own hand

VET

for Cowboy

high noon eyes
the haunt. a deserted street
ghost town/his mind
spurs that jingle jangle jingle

"marry me"

showdown
broadwalk. take it to the bitter end
the shack where cowboy and his uncle dwell among
                    rags and
half pints. whiskey nights behind the wheel glide/ride
freeways/bust broncs
off one ramp on another
hypnotized. glued. burned. stone
over shoulder/eyes eat flesh
gobble up hours in the saddle/garden/sea
skin and bone revolt

World War I
World War II
Korea
Viet Nam

Boot Hill

'merican and proud of it

strong lean earth brown arms lift
corpses from deep river
put gentle in plastic bags

seals them. tags them. each victim
to hole of origin

'round campfire
eyes/photos from the Philippines
"dear mom we eat good. here's my check. tell
everybody hello. this here's me and girlfriend. she
don't speak much english but wes understand things
of import"

black and coolie indian and proud of it

eyes closed. eyes open. eye missing
this shred a child
this worm farm a mother
this crotchless obscenity a man who aspired

on the trail
cowboy in gloves and thigh high boots
fishes
spent flesh from the sea
no six guns. no comanches. no O.K. corral
who in the fuck are the bad guys?

one man against	cement
one man against god	neon
one man indivisible	cash
for justice and liberty	blood

drunk at her door at one AM to get in drunk

hungry for arms lips snapping turtle hungry
her voice/groan/i love you

yes it feels good
to be warm and found

100

round up
stinking rotten remains/unburied affairs
both barrels open he straddles her
gives her the spurs
she's off at a gallop
he works her
rides range: "gonna tame this here pussy"
her corpse/struggle, under him
never mind the maggots/ghosts/loves past

Marine and proud of it

cross the 35th parallel
hot. steam. earth. jungle. rice. sweat
he's never seen insects so big
can't wait to be stateside
will miss the dope
misses his twin brother killed behind enemy lines

who in the fuck are the good guys?

water duck. leatherneck. fool.

bowie knife to her throat he's there/flashed/flipped
slant eyes. gook. 'nese (don't let sundown catchya)

"what'm doin' here nigger in a strange land scared shitless
what the white boy gone'n done now? i don't hate
        these folk"

bowie knife to my throat black gone yellow (they kept him
locked up for a while) what the hell it's all blood it's all
red — my life/his

they put razor blades in their cunts

(soldier, soldier
i declare
i see someone's
underwear
it may be black
it may be white
it may be loaded
with dynamite)

napalm on the streets of laredo
sergeant billy the kid
they make horses of metal that never go lame
steel vultures with radar eyes
agent orange tumbleweed
the school marm carries an M-16 and smokes skagg

rodeo

they have an island for soldiers with exotic diseases

water duck. leatherneck. child

her body floats up to him
he bags it
seals it
tags it
each victim
to hole of origin

sundown
rides off toward
home

war begins

AUGUST 29TH 1970

Ruben they are knockin' in the door

Ruben you better split, man
fast

no. not that way. it's a dead
end

you had no business comin' here to cover the
raza happenings

you know people know they ain't gonna
get the truth
no how

Ruben, you better get outta here quick

man, your woman
she's gonna cry

man, your mama
she's gonna cry

man, your people
they gonna cry

man, they breakin' in the door

they breakin' down justice

man—they sendin' you into *mañana*

DAVID POLION

an 11-year-old boy was fatally wounded one
Sunday night

by a bullet
fired into his home

he was taken to the hospital
pronounced dead. a victim of a drive-by shooting

(the gangsters didn't even know they'd killed him
shootin' away stupid jobless ignorant
hopeless shootin' for kicks)

this 11-year-old Black boy
the same age as my youngest

he was identified by a relative. his cousin said:

>We were in the living room dancing.
>He was standing, watching.
>We heard the shot.
>He ran to the kitchen and collapsed
>and began crawling.

the 11-year-old Black boy
same age same race my son

was shot and killed Sunday night
when a bullet was fired into his home

he ran into the kitchen and collapsed

the bullet traveled a hundred yards
before smashing into the living room. it passed thru
        a window
near the family's recently decorated Xmas tree

he ran into the kitchen and collapsed

an 11-year-old boy was fatally wounded
Sunday night.

a child the same age as my son

and i'm crying
as though i am his mother

BERNADETTE NEXT DOOR

bernadette her shrill terrified wind
bites my ears

outside my glass bernadette stands
a plethora of blood-red plaids against
electrified night

she's trying to get in here. she's trying to
eat up what's left

bernadette the brutish saint
her child licks the dust

the essence of fuckeduppedness

broom rider. halloween as lifestyle
a sickening filthy secret seeking exposé

white flesh her spiked tongue and puke-colored
teeth nasty yellow glints in bleak brown orbs

she's dying to get in here

bernadette. good graves good neighbors make

i'm burning candles against you

FAT

Over skunk, laughter and dago red, me and Kika were jawing with Crystal, the 6 foot, 4 inch caucasian transsexual dope dealer. His three hundred and fifty pounds were hugged up on the couch next to his skinny, redneck, teenaged runaway lover. We were digging on a sitcom and during the commercial breaks, listening to Crystal fill us in on his sex change operation and how wonderful it feels to have a brand new pussy.

The sitcom blipped off and we were stunned by the rude vision of bony African children bent by vitamin deficiencies and social upheavals as their sphinx-eyed mothers with grotesque, juiceless, leathery breasts attempted to nurse husks of babies.

Crystal started the bad mouth. "This looks like Commie propaganda. Look at the women. How come the women don't look so bad. They look fat and healthy to me. Somebody's eatin'," he crowed. "These bleeding heart Christians are a crock of shit."

"It's the diet," I offered lamely, "you can see the same phenomenon in any urban or rural ghetto right here in the U.S."

"The diet?" he laughed. "They're dyin' to eat." His lover joined him in a chorus of belly-shakes. Kika and I stiffened. We are as black as those African mothers and fat has begun to nest around our hips and thighs in like fashion. I tap Kika's wrist and we split, Kika quick on the phony excuse.

"They don't understand the genetic dynamics involved," I bled into her ear as I bogarted the car through heavy afternoon traffic. I was going up in steam. "How our bodies retain mass under threat of famine. How the ability to retain fat is vital to tribal survival. How it helped us get through slavery."

"So *that's* why it's nearly impossible to starve it off," Kika nodded, enlightened.

"Damn it, Kika, that freak had his nerve," I struggled to maintain.

"I know. Simmer down. It's not worth your precious sweat," she said gently and fired the first in a long series of menthol cigarettes.

AMERICAN SONNET (5)

rusted busted and dusted

the spurious chain of plebian events
(aintjahmamaauntjemimaondapancakebox?)

which allows who to claim the largest number of homicides
the largest number of deaths by cancer the largest
number of institutionalized men the largest number of
single female heads of household the largest number of
crimes of possession the largest number of functionally
insane the largest number of consumers of dark rum

largely
preoccupied with perfecting plans of escape

see you later alligator
after while crocodile
after supper muthafucka

CASTING CALL (2)

schemin' and dreamin'

something about Amos. he wore his hat like
an aviator and drove that cab like a dive bomber
scoping in on enemy installations, sported that
jacket with pride debonair, not to mention
he always made good sense

more than Lightning who, i would discover years
later, was merely caught in the act of being himself

more than tall Mr. Andrew H. Brown, foil and
thick-lipped good-natured sidekick whose
dome-lidded bowler was an extension of his head
and there wasn't much in either. his expression of
shock was manifest ugly, an ill-fitting cigar
popping out as his mouth froze into an O

even in black and white i imagined his gums a
pinker blush than Veronica Lake's thighs when she
did a peek-a-boo

the only thing i dug 'bout *Amos 'n Andy*
were the grand opening credits which rolled
across a mock urban skyline to a choir singing
as if in nigger heaven. i'd imagine myself grown up
sitting in a bar, sipping the beer that made
Milwaukee famous, looking fine and dressed to the nines

i never guessed time would
peg me in the hole of Kingfish

110

WHAT HAPPENED IN PEORIA

her quasar lips and video eyes took hold of
his receptors so he couldn't change his channel
he had no choice but to buy a sneak preview
and once one, why not more.
                              he tried his commercial best
to keep programming light and inconsequential but
she had some kind of satellite dish that piqued
his network drawing him into her cinnamon sitcom
a spinoff in live and living color not to mention
she had big production values which he couldn't help
but admire after the fifth or sixth rerun his
series developed an enormous net gross for her
enticing drama.
                    she lured him out into the
game show night against his better judgment. they took
a stretch limo to the drive-in movie and he awoke
hours later shaken rudely by an exploding cathode tube
she had turned a jump-cut with the keys to his hot box

after a hasty search of his mind he found nothing

NO MALICE IN MOVIELAND

in *the business* i can't get the business
even if marvelously stupendously qualified
qualifications aren't at issue
question is can i walk-the-walk talk-the-talk
give good meeting? the fact that i can turn
emotional lead into literary gold (if allowed into
the lab) merely inspires lunch-interview at a tony
bistro or the mere whiff of boardroom neon. close
but no cashier's check. it's not anywhere near
the blatant bigotry previously practiced by
their parents. they like black music and
the moves blacks make. they can even do
the chu berry and the james brown
of course i understand. it's never personal
i'm just not quite what makes the old
socks go up and down

OF APES AND MEN

as we posed around the appetizers, drinks snugged to our lips, in his cozy digs, overlooked by two very thrilling Rembrandts, our host, the successful scriptwriter, bent our interest with an amusing account from his early days

the occasion was the making of a Tarzan sequel. the director had come up with a daring idea: the movie would open with several minutes of beautiful footage as hundreds of apes and assorted monkeys scaled African bush and swung through trees in fierce ecstatic freedom. instead of using the standard canned simian sound track, the director thought it would be much more authentic to strip in the joyous cries of the actual beasts

this remarkable scene would be followed by the majestic appearance of the Great White Ape himself, sweeping triumphantly across the screen, the conceptual genius of having the little critters' actual never-before-done endorsement of the white man as king-of-the-jungle gave everyone hard-ons

elaborate preparations were made. a special sound stage was constructed. the call was put out. animal trainers and their tamed hirsute trainees, from far and near, were flown or driven onto the Hollywood lot and escorted to the sound stage. the lights dimmed in the impromptu theatre and the silent footage unreeled, a slowed-motion spectacle of hundreds of limbs arched in fluid glory, eyes flashing, teeth ablaze

there was an amazing lengthy silence as the clip ended and the lights went up. without prompting the entire room erupted in

113

sudden violence as the startled trainers were attacked by their
charges who brutally clawed, bit, shat and threw feces

•

later, over dinner, he and i began a conversation on the state
of my race

"your people have made a good deal of progress, haven't they,"
our host waved his fork with authority

"on the contrary," i struggled to conceal my outraged astonish-
ment to hear this presumably cultured man utter such bigoted
banalities, "the progress you speak of is quite illusory"

"oh?"

and as i launched an impassioned explication his eyes lost luster.
he rose and abruptly left the table leaving me with my mouth
open

PACE SETTER

baby is it in the stars? did you descend to earth
from convertible cars? how many drinks in how many bars?
baby you dreadlock now? got plenty kinky on your mind
did you get a sign? is that constellation your big behind?
baby is it in the stars?

baby is it in my eyes? how much hell how many guys?
baby you see beyond the veil. is that because
your skin's so frail? maybe it's in your eyes
are you the keyhole to paradise? how many lays
how many thighs? or is it all a big disguise
lies?

baby do you do the do? make every little neurosis
come true? the jungle jivin' hoo juju or am i in for the
royal screw?

i used to be so frank

she yelped and bayed
there was no moon

i told everybody evahthang. i can't afford
the luxury no more
something terrible has happened
makes me sick inside to think about
this terror
and no matter how close you are
i can't share this for fear
should it hurt you
i wanted to be truthful all my days
that can't be. it was easy to be an open door
when there was nothing bad outside
trying to get in

DREAM 549

i leave the house thru the front door
he leaves thru the back

      our dirty little crib its paintings and dust
      jammed with books funked with grease and cat
      hair our nasty little white wooden prison its
      frayed furnishings and roach-ridden appliances
      our sluggish battle for space our constant seeking
      what was just in-hand vanished unexpectedly
      between one of one hundred cracks the ceiling
      threatening to knock in our mule heads

      the many arguments we will have about getting
          out

how do poor people love
especially the poor without God to dignify their union
(my thoughts on my way to work in this illusion)

when i arrive the receptionist tells me i have a call. as i
round a corner hospital halls alter into nightclub walls
and the daring malt-skinned Cuban i met in another dream
finds me in this one, greets me with a kiss to my hand

      "i've deceived you! not a call, but me, myself
      in person. i've come all this way to embrace you"

i'm upset. he doesn't realize i'm married and while
unhappy i'm trying to make do and am not interested in
giving my man motive for homicide. i decide to play
      him off,
keeping fingers and legs crossed

wham. i'm outside, alone, talking to some teenaged
chocolate-skinned gangsters. they are sitting on the curb
with nothing to do. i ask if they'll help me clean
my house for a few extra bucks. they say yes

when we arrive the front door stands wide open as does
the back. thieves have trashed the place taken our
coins my jewelry the appliances (roaches and all) my word
processor. they've overturned all the books and have
                    chopped
up the bookcases. they've smashed his art and have cut the
throats of the cats. our bedroom is waist-deep in the torn
and balled-up pages of my manuscripts

he comes in behind me surveying the damage, screaming
"what's happened?"

"isn't it obvious?" i say

the chip on my shoulder belongs to her

in the pleasure of his knocking it off i see
her in his rage her skin defining my own
with a flick of a wig my hair hers (she wore
them all the time) this game an emotional
cul-de-sac/adrenaline high he grabs her throat
but it's mine he throttles as we spiral
trapped and burnt in our
respective loathings
flesh & blood demands flesh & blood
with a trick of memory i'm his ex-nag
the dusky cliché who gets off on maximum pain
our new love on hold till
he lets go of her

BLUES FOR THE MAN ON SAX (3)

reed-colored lips to mouthpiece

she waits for his attention to turn her way she's
young yet but he lusts for a younger miss snorts
to express his need to re-seed over whiskey fantasy
three-on-a-bed asks her to score like she's bottom
woman or whore to his pimp she balks talks fast
and goes home solo

fingers keys in frenetic flight

at the inner city halfway house for crazies the
elderly tribal princess stammers after the ancient
medicine man in mutual inebriation they trip
his Hopi face the canyon's floor her mesa-high pain
she pushes him up the hall then down, emoting
"be a man! sit down and be a man!"

tenor alto baritone. rapt

she goes for his jugular the ninety pound vamp
thatch of cola wig wobbling her head bobbing
sex-for-punishment even snarls for his crotch those
glossy red lips her teeth threatening castration he
pushes her away and offers up a meal of fists

understated woodwind

they catch him full-saddle riding bitch in heat
wailing "come on mama" in the back seat of the sedan
the city's finest rise out of smog, headlights
shields and handcuffs flashing
no. not rape or public fornication but burglary
to put his bare ass up period

120

FLAWED REPETITIONS

coming here the last time i thought
i'd got it right. here's yet another effort

after rising. the concept of being brought down
and having to struggle to rise again

a well-examined hurt still hurts until the healing
takes. (one not of Assisi)

the exactitude with which the same story is told
with the overly familiar precise mouthings and weary
emphases only vaguely related to the established point
intrusive on an evolving dialogue which might have
concluded in arousing satori but is instead
truncated by the tired reminiscence of something
banal and extraneous

the impatient ego which deftly assumes
anticipates then undermines one less glib

boredom — the inability to appreciate the
subtle aesthetics of deep tight layering

in this dizzy instance i am absolutely still
while the world woogies round me

how many stabs before i pierce his skull?

AMERICAN SONNET (6)

portfolio profligates of creative capitalism
proliferate — wage slave labor intensive

pack up all your cares and dough
here we go interest's low
bye-bye bankbook

pro rata (whacked-out on assonance
and alliteration)

middle management mendacity
(let jesus do it on his lunch hour)

i hit forty before i got my first credit card

zed-to-zed/the game of bird association

when one's only credentials are the holes
in one's tired bend-overs

what does fame do without money?

DREAM 711

i appear at the desk and present my papers

the wheat-colored guard in gray uniform has me sign the register. he points to the elevators. they are spacious and clean. i enter one and press the button and it rises. exiting, i move to my left down cream-colored corridors trimmed in tea-rose and sea green past door after door until i come to an oval reception area. the neatly gray-uniformed woman behind the desk is the color of wheat. she takes my papers and tells me to sit. she goes into the computer terminal and updates my stats. there is an old umber-skinned snaggle-toothed woman strapped on a gurney in the hallway. in garbled croaks she says she must go to the bathroom or else she's going to pee on herself. the receptionist takes no notice. she hands me back the papers and points. i follow her finger, walk past the old woman, and enter a maze of more softly-lit cream-colored corridors. i follow the arrows, avoiding the luminous green exit signs, passing rooms marked "in use" and empty waiting rooms where television monitors air daytime soap opera after daytime soap. i waft along the corridors moving with anticipation.

suddenly the corridor reverberates with the authoritative tenor of an unseen white male droning "you must cooperate if we are going to help you"

the corridor ends in a doorway marked "success." i turn the knob and enter. behind a desk sits a small, bearded, wheat-colored, gray-suited man. idly he fingers a smith & wesson, looks up to see me.

"good," he smiles, "i was afraid you'd woken up"

123

BWANA MOON

the black frazzle i'm worn to writhes
disjointed thoughts/evidence of
sociopsycho imbalance

overly concerned with linkages. simply —
i can't think straight anymore

so poor even grief is a luxury

(what he coulda done about his child
woulda saved me the abortion)

take one greedy gut
slap its face
make it stand in the corner
tan its skinny hairy legs with a switch
promise it renewed vision after
a hasty dinner of leftover bitterness
tell it a kinky secret at bedtime

the shallow man
is filled with words
he chirps like birds a flock of turds

DREAM 820

cracks and dust

in the room's subfusc light i become my shadow
rise above myself to watch my body
brown skin brown eyes my white-toothed yowl
psyche drowning in soma

i stand before me smiling
show me my own hard dying

i look into my old crone face wrinkled the way
i will wrinkle. an old vudun. i wonder
could this be a transmission? am i
doing this

you will die a slow painful death you will

i stare at my bedded self feverish tossing, thin
and twisting she moans my dying she moans my
giving up giving over even as i rage against it

silent screaming i'm seized by
sudden profound disappointment how it can be

you are disqualified for being too good

unfair not fair my whole groping has been slow
and painful slow in achieving recognition painful
in finding love slow in earning money
a failed life

everything will disappoint you. even death

i had hoped

i would be blessed would be one of the quick
of the dead.

i awake to find it is still too early to
get up. i'm angry about that

too

ALL MAPS TELL LIES

measure for yourself. the United States will
fit into Africa times three

and Europe is a much smaller matter than
schoolbooks teach

and being an avid reader of maps is meaningless
with as good an eye as i who study hard study true
i was a scholar of the roads unaware there was
no there to get me there

el dorado was but a path turned back upon itself
my drive endless as i sweat the travel of
this maze dazed i can't figure it. i know i read
it right and yet i'm stranded dead-end after dead-end
endless. my compass ain't worth spit
and the North Star? there's no fix in it

the language of these maps is written
in a secret code not intended for the black of me

all maps lie
and we who take them factually

lost

CRIMINAL BEHAVIOR

i am guilty of not earning enuff money to
raise my children in the style they're accustomed
to seeing on television and in the movies

yes yes

guilty of failing to convince my various
employers i am worthy of a salary commensurate
with my capabilities

guilty of ignoring my bigoted neighbors who spy
on me as i come and go. guilty of never
saying hello good morning fuck off

guilty of refusing to swallow abuse leveled
at me by hostile store clerks who assume i must
be stealing since i fit the ethnic profile
of those born thieving

guilty of having so many lovers before meeting
my last love of needing an excessive amount of
love of loving to be loved of being a lover
of love and once in love working hard loving it

yes yes

guilty of longing desperate want hunger ambition
needy so in need to be someone to shine to stand
out to achieve excellence to be better

as accused i have refused
to feel contrite rebuff the notion of wrongdoing
am willing to pay the price for my assertive

128

stubbornness stick my tongue out in
contempt/flick my finger

guilty

of being self-righteous indignant bold
nasty queenly name-calling and combative

and yes the world owes me

MR. WALTER

she calls to tell me our old associate
the gossip columnist died of the virus

last i saw his bourgeoisie
he was writing a play about mamie pleasant

damn. wasn't he married, i ask. what about
his wife?

i don't know, she says. i didn't
know he dabbled

neither did i, i said, but then
there are other ways of contracting
the virus

i guess, she said.

PREDETERMINATION

for scarcity of marijuana on the streets and in
corporate boardrooms a few heads are saying yes once
more to hard liquor and cigarettes. die-hards have said
yes to junk rock speed designer dope. more wine
than ever is consumed in the name of nouvelle cuisine
there must be more danger to life than mere threat
of extinction *blahzeh blahzeh blahzeh* certainly it's
not nearly enuff to be priced out of existence
one needs to feel one has some bone roll
in the crap of being

even when tain't so

CURRENT EVENTS (2)

the business of the dead is booming

lots of cremations. some burials

many white-owned mortuaries are refusing to handle
those deceased who died of the virus. of course

it means the added expense of extra precautions
to avoid worker contamination by bodily fluids

for black-owned mortuaries the money has
never been so good. bodies coming in
like hotcakes

fresh off the griddle

CURRENT EVENTS (3)

he licks his lips
there's this new thing going on, he broadcasts

you're disturbing a reader

oh, sorry. he lowers his voice. she sharpens
her ears, turns them in his direction

there's this new craze behind all this virus
stuff. kind of a reverse reaction of some sort to
all the dying going around. so many have
lost friends and family

such a shame

but check it out. there's this somber cultish thing—
real strange. people who constantly wear
black. to mourn themselves as well as the others

themselves?

it's weird. they're highly sexed. and they
know what the risks are. they've decided they don't
care. what's life worth if you can't connect. you know,
like some smokers who have lung cancer. they've decided
they're going to go ahead and have unsafe sex and enjoy it.
if they die they die. and that's how they know each other
by wearing black wherever they go, night and day

preposterous

yes, well, but isn't it drama of the highest order?

PRANCING IN MY SLEEP

a woman a worker a black
the demographics of poverty U.S.A.

a politically astute beast
intuitively on time yet

unable to market a break-thru/"coeatus"

now that confession has become blasé
and degree of crime tantamount to media status

what's unexposed?

(where are all the monkeys
who've kicked bananas?)

one might degenerate oneself out of business

when and if

the only danger left is
turning off the light

UCLA GRAFFITI BIO MED LIBRARY

beautiful girl's feet smell good

burn everything British except their North Sea
oil — reunite Ireland

chinga a su madre todos los blanquillos

orientals go home

WHITE
ARYAN
RESISTANCE

made in America. tested in Japan

why do vaginas always smell like star-kissed tuna?

Iraq — the people's army

Q: any hot young students want to see a 9.5 inch
    cock on a handsome 25-year-old transvestite?
A: no good. too big. you have to hold back or
    you'll inflict pain not pleasure.

ROTC out!

why do guys like to eat pussy (girls too)
a) less filling
b) meets minimum daily requirements of $C_{12}H_{22}O_{11}$,
    proteins, essential vitamins and AIDS

U.S. killed hundreds of thousands of Iraqi people

heterosexuality is the result of early childhood trauma

Q: what language is this?
A: you're sniffing the wrong can, stupid

they deserve two more atomic bombs

men are such
immature jerks

do wet dreams come true?

butt tastes good
fuck USC

WORKER (2)

i am the dog they whip all day

my coat the burr & tuft
a snag of mange. don't let me see
the pity in your eye. i bite, will take
your hand down thru to bone
no meaner bitch you've met
before or since

i am the dog that bears the whip

recourse? collared, where
do i run? abandon my brood/flesh i've
borne and sworn to love and feed?
where do i run? to the junk heap? to
chase the sun?

my lot's the cur who takes the whip

a punishment as old as my skin
i wear my burden second to no fur
if not fine, then fit
and my shoulders squared to the strut
and my heat no rougher a rut

beneath the whip

don't touch me till the sting
abates. don't tender me
if you value your hide. this
hate could wear you as well as them
who keep me chained & bound

under the whip

don't stroke me till i've
settled in and licked my wound
and fed the litter. i'm not
cowed will never be
if sad if embittered

whipped

and with each crack
of that demeaning lash
i grit, dig in and take the cash
each task each bite
of leather into my back
i curse and hold
my anger check

and pray for the day dogs dream of

FIGURES OF SPEECH

the squeeze-on

last time the window was broken out
then broken out again. time is the price of a police
report which enables tax deduction

someone has targeted us

and last night they went shopping and simply
took the whole tire off our old fire-snorter
we never know what-or-who's gonna
cold-cock us next

(the gypsy sniggers, "i didn't realize
there was really such a thing. isn't poor jew
an oxymoron? and poor black a redundancy")

we look at each other. i have nothing to say

and it's doled out there
with a portion to be spent here and *oyez*
we mustn't forget proper caloric intake or new sneakers
oops. flash no cash. where'd it go

we look at each other. he has nothing to say

someone has targeted us for the feed
a second sense or second sight

it's just that you don't dare grow old here

as if there's ever been a choice

look. there's nothing
but our intelligent wit

what they taught us in school
those centuries ago

is meaningless now
has the value of zip

TAKIN' A HEAD COUNT

we gather

tome-on-tongue the bad verse of
commiseration. one by one the stars wink shut (so
eventually hebben won't shine thru)
some kind of hushed news spoken prayer-like
the fallen the proper context/respect as we recall
console count and catalogue

get into serious nod

the dead before time the dead by social decree
wasted by degree

(the soap box contains soap. wash
your mind)

we moan. we stomp our terrible prose. express
our woes in the mystic polemics of soul

say oh man oh man

blessed existence
so bleak even light is absorbed

THE AMERICAN URBAN CAMP

The economically stimulated thirst for blood; the unrelenting climate of national apathy and fear was the basic thrust of American society circa 1980.

In and about the 1960s almost 80 percent of the Black population was living in the major "urban centers." From 1973 on, during the then called "Energy Crisis Years" and the awakening "Energy Conservation Movement," Blacks were prevented from increasing their economic class related imitation of non-Black migration into suburban communities. It was during these years of American currency devaluation, spending restraint, inflation, oil shortages and zero population growth that the Black birthrate startlingly increased while that of non-minority citizenry dropped drastically.

There was never any open acknowledgment about the evacuation of the Blacks, i.e., the extermination of the negro people. Few non-Black Americans could afford to recognize the plight of nearly a quarter of their population being slowly, systematically "starved," in the profoundest political/economic sense "to death," and remain respectable. It was the dominant Anglo-Saxon Protestant desire to rid its society of a "darker" people who represented the clear threat of racial extinction.

During these two significant decades Black and non-Black regulations became more and more stringent. Civil Rights reversals took place. Blacks were allowed neither separate-but-equal nor minimally adequate public and/or private education. They were forbidden to excel in almost all professions. No Black was allowed to head a major corporate entity or sit (functionally) on its board of directors. Food could be obtained primarily by the use of Federal food stamps issued through the then Department of Health, Education and Welfare (HEW).

During and following the Viet Nam conflict, greater police and drug inducement activity (the opiate/somnambulant social equations of alcohol, heroin, and the animal tranquilizer PCP popularly termed booze, skagg and angel dust) took place in the Urban Camp and steadily increased throughout the 70s as drugs would become a major issue in the coming decades.

While various historians have pointed out that the oppression of colored peoples was, in part, the responsibility of those oppressed (in their failure to unite against/fight said oppressor), others have labeled the extermination of millions of Blacks as an "inexcusable atrocity."

Black Writers (creative as well as professional—poets as well as journalists) of the period were at the mercy of a tacit proclamation adhered to voraciously (in many instances and subconsciously in others) by television, motion pictures, newspapers and magazines as well as major publishing houses and, to a slightly lesser extent, the art world:

a) Language and literature are the purest expression of a people.
b) There is, at present, an antagonism between American literature and the nature of Black people. This situation is degenerative.
c) Purity of language and literature is our national duty.
d) Our most dangerous adversary in the performance of this duty is the Black.
e) Blacks are only able to think like Blacks. When they "write white" they are lying.

f) We want to root out these lies.

g) We consider Blacks alien and take the characters of our non-Black people seriously. Therefore, we demand censorship: Black works must be monitored. If they appear on television they must appear only in comic or fantastic form. The "Black way" of life must not be allowed to clutter the public air, public libraries or other public communication media.

The dominant culture used every possible means to bring non-Blacks to consider Blacks their great inferiors. Latent anti-Black sentiment was formed into a powerful political weapon. Measures were taken to ban Blacks from further participation in the dominant American society, condemning Blacks to hopeless economic struggle and inevitable death in the subculture of the Urban Camp.

Approximate number of victims
of the major Urban Concentration Camps:

Atlanta, Georgia	50,000	bergen-belsen
Jackson, Mississippi	92,000	ravensbruck
Miami, Florida	63,500	buchenwald
San Francisco/Oakland, California	70,000	dachau
New Orleans, Louisiana	138,000	mauthausen
Houston, Texas	74,000	flossenburg
Seattle, Washington	35,000	theresienstadt
Boston, Massachusetts	100,000	sachsenhausen
Harlem/New York City	2,000,000	auschwitz
Washington, D.C.	1,380,000	maidenek
Chicago, Illinois	600,000	belzec
Philadelphia, Pennsylvania	280,000	sobibor
Los Angeles, California	731,800	treblinka
Detroit, Michigan	600,000	chelmno
Newark, New Jersey	67,500	stuthof
Puerto Rico	2,350,000	
Jonestown, Guyana	934	

144

NOTES OF A CULTURAL TERRORIST (2)

after the war the war begins the war goes on

i am a soldier. look at my boots
soles worn from seeking work. from hours
in unemployment lines

call me a civilian casualty

the war to feed children the war to clothe their backs
the war to meet the rent the war to keep the gas tank
        full the
war to end the calculated madness keeping the poor poor

what happens to a war deferred
does it implode? does repressed aggression
ravage the collective soul?

(there's rioting now. i see the blaze red smoke rising.
the city burns. people are looting, taking things. all the
excess denied them. crimes of possession. to have. without
the onus of color or fear of rejection. children carry racks
of clothes. women push shopping carts brimming with food.
men favor liquor stores and gunshops. but what we need is
revolution. bloodless or otherwise. we must go deeper than
lust gratified in one spontaneous torrid upsurge of rage)

i am a soldier. look at my hair
fallen out under stress. the many hours
unappreciated on the job. not even a decent chair

call me collateral damage

and when all the foreign battles are won

will we who battle here at home
have our day in democracy's sun?

(i am laying on the gurney in the hallway. there
aren't enough beds. he's been here with me for hours and
we came in last night. and they still haven't been able to
tell us anything. they wanted money up front before they
even talked to us. luckily we had assistance but still had to
borrow from mama to make the cash co-payment. the pain is
real bad and i'm thirsty. but they said not to drink anything/
nothing by mouth. and we had to wait forever just to get this
far. too many patients and not enough doctors)

i am a soldier. but my back is broke
battling the papers i push all day. my hope
is broke too. how do i love

call me politically correct

(we sat in the bar in the late afternoon trying to figure out
where all the men had gone. the ones that weren't dead or
in jail. who loved women. the ones who weren't junkies
weren't alcoholics weren't already married. the ones who
love our color. and one sistuh took a tall swig and said
she'd be satisfied if she lived to see her refrigerator full
just once before she departs this planet)

what happens to a war deferred
does it seep down into the skin a rash
of discontent to erupt again and again?

i am a soldier. that i live is a lie
no one stares 'cuz no one cares. grasping
for a nip of pleasure a toke of sanity

call me a victim of victims

146

(the cuffs are tight. i can feel them rubbing against my
wrists behind my back. we're taken out to the squad car
in front of all the neighbors. the kids stare at us. they
knew we were different all along. we didn't belong in this
'hood. he's angry. he wants to know who ratted. i can't feel
anything but numb. they shove him into the back first and
then i climb in behind him. it's a short drive to the
precinct. we're broke. we'll have to borrow money for
bail. we're about to find out who our real friends are)

whatevah you do
don't look me too long in the eyes

we could've made it if

i were flat
and you were round

you slept on your left side
and i on my right

you had the eyes of an iguana
i had the lips of a rose

you had been born under libra
i had been born the year of the tiger

if you were the loch and i the fathomless
creature of your depths if

your touch were as soft as your eyes
my flesh were as hard as my heart

i licked the salt from your neck
you licked the salt from my wound

you were my monkey
i were your jones

if

you were taller
i were brighter-skinned

A NIGGER'S VOICE FEELS CURIOUSLY COOL

— after e. e. cummings

your favorite authors never knew the thou of you
and when you come across your image in the pages
of their lore a shitting horror takes hold

      "this ugly reference is to me" words
      with no affectionate (intelligent at least?) context

cut

      effect/a bleeding from your literary butt

negro negress niggah without redress
lynched by the very literacy you aspire to embrace
erased and rewritten a badly conceived footnote or hasty
addendum in the prissy history of a given humanity

dat dey luvz jazz or blues does not excuse dem

rage and rage and rampage again
those tomes stand silent on the shelves themselves
witness to impotent fury they got their got
and your goat too

as you cringe before the failings of writers
of your native skin and tongue wishing off them and you
the stench of English dung

no wonder in your neighborhood
libraries are tombs

and you you lover of the word
hang yourself from the stacks

DREAM 1031

in terror i wake but can't rise

the long dark is filled with fierce shallow wind.
i'm in our bedroom, its glut of books, the ceiling fan,
the white levelor blinds, the faint pungency of scented
candle wax. i am sprawled on the bed (yet the floor)
and feel a warm wetness oozing into my groin.
alerted, i know someone else is in here. he's finished.
he's turned to go. i see his assassin's back. i know
he conceals the beretta. there's a thin gray cowl
cloaking his head. he wears black slacks and a salmon
pink-on-black silk paisley shirt which ripples against
the ess of his back in the shrill wind. i know his back. i
think to cry out a warning to my lover but realize
i'm weighted to the floor (now the bed) beneath his body.
there's a bullet in his head at the temple and a bullet
has pierced his upper torso beneath his heart. he lies
across my chest, bearded mouth slack and open. i hear
the yowl of wind. i remember how death felt in the
cold hand of my father. but if we've been murdered
in bed (yet here on the floor) aren't i dead also?
then how do i think?
                    abruptly i re-awake to discover
someone has tiptoed into the room and has clicked off
the television set

WHALES

as gods — so-called
primitives once worshipped them they ruled
earth sea

now disease now parasites now pollutants —
a complexity of environments
many die of no apparent cause
they produce fewer and fewer young

unexplained mass beachings

attempts at rescue/prevention/preservation
fail

it is surmised the "superior" intelligence
of a species

is measured by its acceptance of

its time having passed

THE SYSTEM

something there is that insists
i stay outside in this unforgiving dark

i demand entry, i declare

you won't be permitted. not in
this life, it retorts
and it is the only life you have

then
i'll spend my life trying

waste your life if you want

then what do you suggest

that you adjust to your status
accept it

i can't. i want in

then it will be seen to that what
you want is valueless if and once
attained

•

angrily i charge the door
it spins. outside again

AMERICAN SONNET (7)

to take the outer skin in. rehumanize it

is

swallowing whole the dourness of
an unremitting scorn and unstoppable cruelty
the exploitive ambition of pricey looks
stealing meat off the bone

is

to know grief my unnaming tongue
it reaches for its lyric the mother of
all pain to birth to know this ugly/an
abandoned stillborn blued around its eyes and
bodily bruised. found buried in a dumpster
beneath the rages of an unsung life

is

to know i must survive myself

Part 3: But ambidextrously . . .

BONES

throw them
and they come up with the certainty
of a too tight skin

do them
and the consumptive habit will
possess what available future
there is

wish upon them
snapping with ease as they promise
wisdom wealth and escape

turn them
and discover rich ancestry/feed
for a hunger so deeply black

it's right down to them

IN A NEAR EMPTY ROOM

peach-on-peach walls and linen tablecloths
the gin and tonic meets bourbon straight
with club soda back. we catch the late set
Clark Terry and company at the bar and grill
where Joan is an original tune

this time of greats passing a generation of
trumpets laid to rest of pianos in decline

say little man jazz come blow your horn
the moon's in the west and the news forlorn

where are all the comers? slaving part-time
days to keep themselves in notes

MEANWHILE IN MANHATTAN

bad sushi

the future takes a bullet. on the A-train up from
Atlantic City we escape coal-stained urban granges/the
backwashes of failed industries and polluted truths. we
head north on the overground railroad seeking

the mythical pouch of his gestation/stone mother gargoyle
whose million-nippled breasts eternally nurse
the skyline arms extended in the gritty girth of her
tortured promise. we enter at Penn Station greeted by
shit-stained stumblers in shadow spurring the unreachables
on with croaks of "spare change"

my name password for excitement

we have come here à la crusade to find and confront—
mission irascible make some kind of connexion
between then and now when and how (seek and deplore)
his long mink hair streaming behind him i trail him in my
sleepwalk our soon-to-be-aborted child a pernicious hunger
denying me sleep—our stillborn success

steel papered in major and minor agonies the cacophony
of light bulbs shattering in street lamps *zzzttt* of the
red hotel neon sign peeping thru torn oilcloth window
          shades
the blessed hum of elevators zinging upward to
righteous oblivion or plunging downward to "where the
par-tay's goin' on" or

my name is woman-has-no-mind-left

next the ritual of exchanging banalities over expensive
cheesecake that's thick cool porous and flavorless
knowing secretly it's run by a corrupt union
even sweetness is on the take. but Empire State is still
full-flower the Flatiron Building as wedged and flat
Central Park is central to the point as ever even if
Ms. Statue of Liberty has taken hiatus for a skin bleach

(i wonder when i'm gonna see that massive sea of white
flesh congesting cement from 42nd to Wall Streets — all
those gentlemen blondes prefer. all i see are niggahtoes
or variations on dark ethnics down-home uptown Blacks
from Africa, Indonesia, the Bahamas, West Indies, Fiji —
Buddhaheads and Spics — it's all *us* as if the Conk has
either become extinct or taboo)

holy mackerel my name chanted from Brooklyn's bridge

we hole-up in a high-rise war zone where the shell-shocked
and renegade reconnoiter marking time with speculations on
spurious victory. we bribe the guard with forged
                    prescriptions
hiding our insolvency rather well. if only we had a criminal
conspiracy to tighten our game if only we lived as boldly
as we hope if only we had that killer distingué

my name is bitch-don't-you-understand

in latter-day rain all cabs are occupied by petite well-heeled
gray ladies busily plotting the overthrow of night-blooming
muggers. we hail and are stymied we hail and are stymied
we hail and he madly dashes for The Last Taxi on Earth
but Joe Senior stops him jousting and jostling for the ride
as i climb over them into it and send old Joe sprawling
with my booted feet

160

unkosher wine in bag we visit the studio of the Sculptor-of-
Breasts for a crash course on Jewish Holidays. then we
drop in on a cadre of word banditos crammed into a
junked-up den on the kinky outskirts of literacy/crib of his
third birth. challenged to defend the steatopygia typifying
women of my race i explain it eliminates the need for
pillows during sexual intercourse

my name is Sorceress of Muntu

we spook squid tanks in Chinatown, Fifth Avenue
patisseries, the crawls of SoHo, Hudson Riverside haunts.
we dig the fabled Chelsea and the profane Dakota. (we
Ham it up in Harlem in front of the Apollo/photo/me on
his lap/we're immortalized in wicker. we eyeball the
East Village, Christopher Street crannies, then Little
Italy where hostile ebony winos armed with squeegees
demand quarters

he spits my name/a wad of ill-chewed stuff

during his flip-flop there's nuthin' for me to do except
eat and see the sights. history takes hold. George
Washington squatted on the high-priced hole where i
discover All-American sesame flatbread. later i will be
found glass-deep in the 20-inch video watching greed
images set in miasma while uptown he frantically strip-
searches new-age social workers for contraband fatherhood

emotions held hostage our visit to Egypt at the
Metropolitan is a jizzmic rush/twenty-six galleries of
archaeological theft/my ancient blood-ties i fight the urge
to genuflect fight my tongue it seizes his/we ignite necking
among gold artifacts scarabs and urns our only wealth
a rich mutual insatiable lust

my name a whisper at twenty after midnight

underneath it all urbane garbage rages the rot of
       unresolved
dilemmas hearts rubbed raw toothy flea-ridden fears nesting
behind skin-thin walls the sewage of naked neuroses
rising wind-chill factor dealing in hallucinogens
smirking visions dancing on the third rail. bad sushi

my name is more than he'll ever know

feeling
gives birth to
movement

ESSAY ON LANGUAGE (3)

lately i make sacrifice
in terms of sweat

      what is the meaning of my thirst?

there are cookie jars
and there are cookie jars

      how do i enter apart from myself?

the alabaster sentinel before the doorway
halts ascension. "mama sweet mama don't go"
but i'm so torn so worn so full of scorn
having exhausted reality so thoroughly

      will it call on me again?

how many years in stir
for fronting off truth as fiction

      where is the spark that promises stars?

interference/red noise of pre-sex a sonorous
breathy licking of licker he makes like a dragon
some beast deranged by a prolonged case of
blue balls

      who is in my blood?

funny thing about lingoes
death is to be fluent in them all

AR'IOCH

disguised as a man he made his way into her
bed. settled near the window overlooking the apricot
sapling. before she allowed him in he had to promise not to
touch her. he would remain true to his word as long as
necessary. keeping very still he pretended to be
interested in television while she slipped into
a gown, turned off the lights then crept into her side
of the bed. he anticipated completing his seduction
inevitably taking advantage of her nature since a
working woman always offers comfortable concealment. this
one was not bad for looks her good fleshy musk like mother
never was

ALL OF THAT

— after Aaron Shurin

she woke to find the pillow strapped between her
legs and no memory of how it got there.
was it Hegel or Heidegger? Kafka or Malraux?

she found the closet door difficult to open and
steadily jerked the knob. in seconds she was
teen-aged, popping the fingers of her left hand
and getting down those bop steps

(do the spirit-walk do the spirit-walk
wiggle and squiggle and jiggle when you talk)

smoothly skillfully exhaustively researched
his huge purpose entered into her reluctance
it was savage. he split her sensibility in two
later she would discuss the ramifications
with a girlfriend over espresso

head in hands she dwelt on the details of
her resume. she was making too much sense. it
was time for a semi-drastic change. tragedy lay
in her preoccupation with the soprano staccato
of her own breathing

when the door finally opened
she was assaulted by the odor of toe jam
stinky sneakers and socks standing at attention
without the benefit of feet

DREAM 1218

i snap out of my distraction and hurry from the
                bus and
realize i overshot the melrose exit. it's a cold
                clear winter's
night and i'm stranded on a Hollywood street corner
                lights on
buildings and marquees make my eyes feel brand new
                people are
going about their commerce, in and out of buildings
                and numerous
construction sites. i'm freezing, no coat, and
                anxious to
get home. i seek out a phone booth and begin dialing
                frantic

actually i'm at a casual affair and am immensely
                enjoying
my dance with a guinean gentleman. he is very polite
                and makes no
moves. the music stops. he thanks me, then escorts me
                over to a
quiet corner where he introduces me to a British
                Shakespearian
actor. we begin chit-chat

still dialing i can't get through i can't get through
                i'm tired
i want to go home and wonder how long it'll take me to
                hoof it
maybe twenty minutes. after a few persistent rings he
                answers
sleepily distant. *he's been napping again,* i think
                angrily, then

ask him to come pick me up and he says, yeah, of course
        where are you?
i look around for street signs and say, the corner of
        Selma and
Hill. he doesn't understand. "Where's that?" i
        repeat it
anxious over our apparent miscommunication. to
        complicate
matters the vista begins to shift as i talk. suddenly i'm
        at the
corner of Fountain and Nietzsche, then La Brea and Sunset
        which is easy
for him to find. he yawns, "Okay" and i hang up, still
        angry, waiting

i decide i may as well walk to keep warm and am suddenly
        joined by the
British Shakespearian actor and Kat, my old runnin' buddy
        from twenty
years back. they appear out of thin air to accompany
        me with chit-chat
and we're suddenly home which is my parents' house
        Kat and the
actor bid me farewell and vanish as my lover comes
        out on the
porch surprised to see me. i cuss him for not
        coming to
pick me up. the car is still parked in the driveway
        he has no
excuse and no apology

then we're in the laundry alcove next to the washing
        machine
which is rapidly filling with hot water. i'm preparing
        the wash when
my lover comes over to kiss me. i attack him, knocking

                    him to the
floor with the weight of my body. i begin to bury him
                    head first
in his own pile of dirty shirts

i awake, my eyes focused on the levelor blinds. it is
                    raining. i
remember the letters i forgot to mail yesterday

WANT ADS

40% of women who separated recently while
in their 30s will never remarry

long straight hair that hangs to the small
of the back hangs to the hips dimples
to the ankles gets in his face when
she's on top

nor will about 70% of women who separated
when older than 40

flies in autumnal wind. jostles
and bounces with each confident step
mirrors sunlight. the youthful stuff sonnets
and prayers are made of

altho 72% of recently separated women will
eventually go to the altar again, half will be single
seven years after the split

silk that hides the modest maidenly pubis
inspires the bridal train
represents tresses. 100 strokes of the brush
to keep it glistening and tangle free

a 46% remarriage rate for black women contrasted
with 76% for white women

no kinky snarls

racial differences have been found before
but the reasons
are not understood

moon goddess/the less that is more

EATER OF GOOD BOOKS

each word each syllable
repast

at the table i am alone
they will come sit here many times
i will never be quite here again
flanked left and right yet alone
at the table
eating hale yet tasting nothing but tart ripe bitterness
my own meat its deepening blackness though
all one might see is brown
at this table surrounded by ghosts (no they are flesh
and blood, blue veins throbbing in white, it is i who am
of an *other* world)
eating and silent stilled and stymied
by the formal nature of my haste
i can't afford a minute away from myself
must be more alone if possible
(the loneliness of a scorned race, poets or negroes, you
understand that—of course you do. i can't be alone
in that) alone in my youth alone in my age alone
in my truth

certifiable. yes

i survey my plate portion out each various bite
in perfect ratio
a splash of blues of tears of reaching thru time
to heal the wounded womanchild i am

fear and pain
with which i salt-and-pepper
to savory excess

170

(i can no longer afford that kind of solitude

and the streets that gave me shape have been long
torn up, repaved)

i am sick and starved to death among the resonance of
rhythms i will never taste again (which is why i'm
always reluctant to brush after meals)

fat on the rich yet unfulfilling

UNFINISHED SCRIPT

A woman's scream is heard followed by a series of moans.

Fade in is also the turning on of a lamp which sits on the bed-stand in the bedroom of elderly Mr. & Mrs. Elmore Ashworth. It has been turned on by the anxious Dora as she rigidly sits listening to the alternating cascade of half-cries and whimpers as they penetrate the bedroom wall. She turns to her soundly sleeping husband and shakes him.

> Elmore! Elmore! He's beating her again!
> Do something!

Elmore groans and turns over.

> Mind your own business, Dora!

He turns his back to her, burying his wispy-haired head in the pillows. She lifts the phone from its cradle and aggressively punches the touch-tone tabs.

> I'm calling the police!

CUT TO

Exterior corridor of the adjoining apartment. Angle on the door as two black-clad uniformed officers approach, combat-ready. Officer A takes up position on the right, Officer B on the left. Officer B readies his club then uses it, banging loudly against the hardwood door.

172

Open it up in there. Police!

After a beat the door swings open. A tall, very hairy, very well-muscled Jewish male in his late 40s stands defiantly butt-naked in the entrance. The two officers exchange a look. Officer B clears his throat officiously.

> We got a domestic violence complaint,
> mister. Neighbors say you're beating
> your wife.

The man smiles, defiant and sarcastic.

> That's right. So arrest me already.
> I'm beating her with this.

He shows off his still-erect, grossly over-large circumcised penis as the officers vacillate between annoyance, disgust, amusement and laughter.

NERUDA

few quiet hours
i spend them soaking in the tub with my neruda

in a dream a bearded moreno stranger
approaches me along a dark street in the plaza
as we pass he whispers hoarsely, "neruda"

on sunset boulevard a beggar accosts me
for spare change. i hand him my collected neruda

while my lover takes siesta i walk down to
the neighborhood bar for a game of pool solo. i order
dos besos. i put a quarter in the juke and notice
all selections read neruda

while standing at the supermarket checkout stand
i read tabloid headlines. one screams
"man force-feeds wife neruda"

(he tells me he is worried neruda is coming between us)

note found in cantonese fortune cookie:
neruda slept here

SOUTHWESTERN SOUL

trucker stops. vanishing points. mirages
old smokey honky joints the leavings of lost tribes
ghosts of cattle drive trails rusted rails of
southern pacific remnants of route 66 bleak
skeletons of Burma Shave signs a surfeit of
turquoise arrowheads and calamity janes

road after road after road

white line fever and a haunted longing
rockabilly turbo thrust from Bakersfield to Nogales
open country open heart and a raw dog moon

here a gray-eyed hate as deep in earth
as dinosaur bones
here a lust as greenless as heat-blown
as rattlesnake shed

i am afraid to raise my hood

sun dance on my windshield. Patsy Cline & Johnny Cash
the wind threatens sandstorm outside Needles
on this drive into the void known as nowhere
heaven is a cow town cheeseburger medium well
apple pie à la mode and steamin' hot java

here. a multitude of baked shit-colored bungalow doors

behind each salvation is stranded

LIKE LOVE (2)

they could be heard thru the walls

making commotion
he'd stick his button in her face
and she'd nail it with a sledgehammer
or she'd come in tired and depressed
and he'd start workin' her nerves or start
to pitch and whine and she'd resent his childish
display and refuse a motherly response

evoking his instant anger and
recollection of similar mistreatment by another
ex-past arousing her ire she's sick of being constantly
compared against the fluctuating vista of old fucks
then he stabs her a second time before the first
wound bleeds

now they're beating dead metaphors
and slinging choice epithets and if he touches
her she's gonna destroy the one thing he regards
as precious and he restrains his fist threatens to
leave her because hasn't she seen her body lately
and other women look at him constantly

she invites him to go on out there and
get whatevah crotch-rot they's givin' up these days
and stymied he hugs it in and exits to her screams
curtaining the wall between them as he slams the door

HECUBA ON SUNSET (2)

i went to the well to wash my toe

traversing the backside of Vermont in my usual snit
loaded down my purse my thermos my notebooks the
weight of my hate my brain-rotting job the weight
of my anger at social injustice the weight of
survival worries as i jaywalk the street

behind the burger stop a high yellow man in his 30s
in dayglow hard hat, candy-apple red shirt and beige
corduroys sits on the wall next to the parking lot
he eats from the deep olive drab industrial garbage
bin. as i pass him i'm stunned by the fierce slam
of a cold baked potato against my head thrown with
full force of his wrath. i burst into pain-shocked
tears and turn to confront him as he explodes in
a patois of yells

"ya killed mah daughter! ya killed mah daughter!"

i smell his blood monkey and decide to deny him
orgasm. for weeks after i wonder what set him off.
my hospital identity badge? was his dead child a
figment of advanced schizophrenia? was i an
unsuspecting double of his brute torment?

what time old witch?

SAPPHIRE AS ARTIST IN THE WORLD

—after William H. Gass

The work such woman does in the world works
on her . . . her movements her perceptions her loves. Life is
intolerable in a society that does not value/want her gift; especial-
ly when it does not want the vision she must espouse in the act
of putting herself in the world thru art. What does Sapphire
envision? Her innate loveliness of which she may be defensive
or insecure. But if she seeds her self-doubt in a nurturing self-
love she may harvest the rapture of creation. Otherwise she may
fill herself with hate, but will her skin contain it? Hate blurs.
Certainly she cannot create when her vision is blurred/out-of-
sync/arhythmic. Rhythm is a state of concentration so complete
it leaves her defenseless, opens to all in tune with it. Intonation
is her other means/meaning into sensation by which her faculties
embrace/subvert. To achieve satiation upon embracing she must
see the world she enlarges (with her art) clearly if not without
fear. She is its lover and she must excite it until its richness rises
in response to her Afro-centric beauty perceived at last. To open-
ly hate and fear her lover is to invite rape. She must see the
hardness in the blood, yet recognize the hardness as required
for effective penetration/dialogue. Therefore she is the natural
enemy of social oppression/impotence. She resists the aesthetic
softness of a society that would sublimate/smother her spirit.
In this context her subversion is catholic, but given sufficient
direction/education her willfulness undermines everything false
with exacting precision. In the end her society will reject or even
destroy her. History is clear on this point. To insure her place
in the world Sapphire must make her art her revolution. And

in so making she must remain undaunted, without compromise. She must be aware of the power which extends thru her bones, the profound stubborn belief in the absolute importance of her vision.

DREAM 5272

manchild and lover in tow, i
revisit a mindscape/lead our run down
corridor after corridor. my son keeps up
but my lover complains, "you're moving too fast"

then he
stumbles and drops to one knee
"i've caught two bullets in my head," he sobs
"it's all your fault for being in such a hurry."

i wonder. was it the man with the beretta?

as my guy collapses, i rush to his side, hug
his head to my heart. an official doctor's voice
announces he has two hours to live if
we don't get him to the hospital quick

my son and i
lift him to his feet. like zip my lover
is in swaddling clothes, arms bared, dark chest
hair exposed against red-white skin, eyes closed
in a faint. like zap the hospital bed swerves into
focus. he's in it, eyes staring upward and away
mouth slack, face expressionless. the ash-blonde
nurse fluffs his pillow, gives me a hostile stare
and tells me to shove it

"he doesn't want you," she says. "he's angry"

i bogart my way to his side only to discover
the sickbed has become a giant bassinet. he's
changed into a cuddly little brown monkey stuffy

with glazed button peepers, a tiny red-and-white
beach ball sewn into his mitt. he can't move
but his toy-eyes clitter with fury

no time to examine my horror

like zooey
i'm in the casino, wading thru the fleshy bodies
of elderly white women and their disgruntled
cow-fed spouses. i'm looking for my beloved
when up ahead

i spy Pop shuffling in, out
and around, arms at his waist, steady swinging
forward and back the way we used to do when we
played choo-choo train

i break the applause meter. he's the way he was
a couple of years after surgery, clad in his
ragged white polyester pj top over baggy old navy
blue slacks barely held up off his behind by
those tired old brown suspenders, the elastic
top of his white undershorts doing a peek-a-boo

he turns and beckons. i remember.
he's dead

rudely, the alarm does its buzz
my sweetheart rises beside me
and hits the disrupt

"time to get up," he yawns, falls
back into the sheets and buries his head
under the pillows

LIFE AS A CARTOON

(you can't use that phrase
someone's already made it fa-fa-fa-famous)

ink peepo

in the mean mean the hip white dress glove
pens the life and times of a modern day female ink spot
(communication via balloon is severely limiting)

inky stinky kinky dinky

panel 1:   stick figure orating
before throng of enthused listeners

panel 2:   stick figure pulled over to curb by
cop and ticketed

panel 3:   2 stick figures fucking
furiously at motel

panel 4:   lone stick figure sprawled helplessly
pinned to earth by giant dollar sign

caption: the way to a stereotype's soul is thru clichés

drippin' off da page

panel 1:   stick figure clinging desperately
to tree limb in hurricane force wind

panel 2:   stick figure with huge heart with crack in it
alone on a beach. tears jumping out knot of
head

panel 3:   stick figure with bandage on heart
            standing in front of mirror

panel 4:   stick figure flattened in wake of
            steamroller

caption: is there happiness after a nite of man wine
            & song?

(who goes there? the slink? it doesn't matter how many
        times
i'm cut, i bleed ink)

NOSOMANIA (3)

no getting in on the ground floor
start with TNT at the foundation

                    this is the program. enter the system here

the root causes of restlessness

characterized by sacrifice
voluntarily stepping into the grinder

cog trauma

you are not supposed to betray your penchant
for melodrama. you are to remain stoic yet
functional and fuckable. no deviations
from the routine. dinner as usual. don't forget
to set the alarm

excessive iffing   the day before it happened
                 i looked down and saw this star
                 it was twinkling there
                 and i knew it was just for me

pink is the color i banished from my wardrobe
the day i overheard father say he
wished i'd been born a boy

FOR ME WHEN I AM MYSELF

the enhanced storage of mother-fat
ancestors subjected to long periods of
deprivation
the body adapted/the generic coding of
racial survival—all dat buttah jigglin' rhythmically

breasts/earthen cups ends up, out towards
(the mirror) aureolae the wet slick sea-brown of kelp
nipple raised to tongue

an essentially hairless desert plain
passion's eyes follow the horizon
at the mouth of my Y one hundred tiny men stand
in militant salute, fists high in the air

skink os opens/patiently takes in satisfaction
nearly the same size as the thang
devouring it
the intense red subject of censorship & social myths
making revelations subversive acts (mingusing)

anatomically other than. yielding looseness
to hot hands. seldom subdued by clothing

who needs the safety of night who finds comfort in the
suggestion of the unexplored

> only love could want this body
> wanting guarantees love

nasty words

visitations/
interaction with
others
leading to an
essentially
negative
catharsis or
exo-cannibalism

(i married my first taste — a mistake coming from hunger, a
discussion centering on the negative images of black
        females as
prospective mates and the related issue of the availability of
men-of-color beyond age twenty-five, balls intact)

der die das die

the car. the driver. sirens. done did do wrong
juvi baby
they will strap you down and take the idea by force
handcuffed, you will not be allowed to nurse or nurture
(what think tanks are for)

whispers outside windows down alleys suggesting (i repeat)
danger even in broad daylight
gangs of shadow, some with toothpicks, a swagger
and ear-splitting funk

watts dreams of dim-lit dingy walkways (i repeat)
dirt-laden drama, linoleum worn thru to floorboards
and across the way the old honky whore gives it up
to the local boy virgins (a first taste of white meat)

all you have to do is be there
be in trouble

the wrong place
quarter slots & computerized victims
revenge and/or initiation killing aka "wasting"
as in "i wasted a couple of mushrooms"
as in video game parlance

the granite white sleepwalk of urban boredom
long blocks of squat stucco housing
liquor lockers, pawnshops, the promise of early closings
(fear sets curfew)
skin scraped raw by the hasty removal of diamonds
set in gold

brown kinks matted and wet—a crown of thorns
exactly (pete & repeat)

not feeling
but the complete lack of it

sinew drawn break-tight at the jaw, neck, forearms
legs set for running at
a whiff of the law
of course you're guilty, you were born
weren't you?

　　　—when ah get to hebben gonna kick off mah shoes—

the accent of broad proper bourgeois vs the broken lingo
of defiant ones/ideological idiots (godfathaless)
rampant romantic notions of nobly dying in the cause
of leaving one's mark (mere graffito to be
whited over)

resulting from industrial detumescence and subsequent
　　　　withdrawal

cool = the ability to maintain absolute equilibrium
       under extreme adversity

hip = recognition of one's disadvantage
       and intellectually compensating to the
       point of reversal or neutralization (at least)

today i am uncool and unhip

beneath the underdog

i hate this space. i am sick of dust. i want clean beige
      walls. i
want solid oak bookshelves. i want cush chairs. i want
      the cats
running free in the garden. i want the rent paid months in
advance. better yet, my own home. i want the old car
      cherried out.
i want a real credit card

who do i rob? (rerun rerun)

my friend the suicide sends her key
that i may drop by anytime

night visits to the rich instead (hebben hebben)
they want to know what neighborhood i live in
who i am
in their assertion of the digestibly universal
they offer up a wrinkled sex, my
power is in knowing i possess it
with or without display
those haints who cling to youth
are their own hell

sing the gospel of mobs and money barons

188

can't say it enuff loud enuff
bellicose witness to crises on-going
plunder & assassination
spew forth testimony — preach
how they scare. how they enslave
yet negate even that minimal work-animal value

A PERSONAL HISTORY:

papa left Little Rock when buck hunting
season started. one was guilty just being there
just being black being male
he knew his temperament
and saw himself hung in the sad young
man strung up in front of the church
as warning to the uppity
promise to the niggerish
his aunt had sent fifteen dollars
for train fare to Chicago, maybe, but
that afternoon he saw a car with
California license plates
and made Los Angeles in time to catch
the earthquake of '33

mama took the train out of Hennessey
domestic jobs opened out west
during the war. white men were
answering the call. their women took
their places in factories and
boardrooms. black hands were needed to
cook clean clothe and feed the young
she worked for the movie star
Ronald Reagan and his wife Jane
but quit after a year because they
refused her a raise
and she didn't like it the time

Lou Costello got drunk and
chased her around the kitchen table

they met in me and another three

•

dear one,

expect this letter to go unmailed as have all the others. i
can't bring myself to send them. i should never write when
angry or depressed. my words seem to overwhelm
              whomever
i write to at the time. i need to write it, so i do, and
tear it up afterwards and go on about my usual struggle
as best i can. writing an exorcism blah blah blah. i imagine
my letter read. and even though it isn't, i feel better
having written, as though it were read and
understood. going thru the process

i'm not good at explaining how i
feel. i have
run out of synonyms for rage

there are preconceived notions in which i feel trapped
i keep thinking my work will liberate me from them

it hasn't

as though life's language is its own snare

so by not sending
these letters i escape entrapment

you dig?

ever so sincerely—

•

regionality = living room

i am, at last, content to leave
the place i've never been
knowing i will never get there

gonna kick off my blues

hostile love

he shuffles the deck expertly. he offers a cut
as if i had a choice. i pass. what difference
can i make? the sonofabitch has memorized the position
of every bloody card. i play the game, my heart jittering,
fiercely stubborn against my calculated loss (karma? *please*)
he smiles as he goes down "the winner"
then coos, "congratulate me"
then tempts me to murder, his mouth twisted in
you act so niggerish. there i go there i go there
i go smashing things glasses shattered wine spilled plates
dashed to the restaurant floor. i rush out into the tony
night to walk it off. waves of crises (for the worse) as his
eyes follow with U-boat acuity

how can he disrespect the millions
whose dying gave us ourselves

no forgetting no forgiving
(cooling out my crazed and exploded flesh)

i go for a reading. the gypsy is tipsy
tells me she needn't fear work. she got enuff moolah
to coast five years and there's always her mama's mansion
in the right white part of town. as for my future? i
shouldn't bank on it

                    not forgotten not forgiven

the dark heart slum effluent
emetic for the bile of spirit

the dark heart broken, spreading
plague. a need-fever (springing from the cavity
of greed. the seat of the great gold-toothed mouth
yawning — its own void/emptiness)

                    the gotten the given

an eeling pain sharp then diffuse
thru gristle then meat

corkscrewing

the dark heart/earth casts up its dead
breathes
the exalted spasm
[my pearl to his tongue
he imprisons/keeps me in its pleasure
throbs moving thru me
his eyes tasting for my sweetening signaling
tabes dorsalis/meltdown]

memory: paper warped by the humidity of
          pressed flesh

                    forgiven not forgotten

we rain in each other/darkness parts
sighing smiling he withdraws from me night after
year after

grabbing tissues to catch our excessive moistures
then

he sits at my side, at the edge of our
storm-wrecked bed

i watch him watch me

(the better) in hazy after-sex
one maverick wisp of hair dangles free at his
sweaty brow, his head tilted slightly
eyes stroking mine in luminous night

as i

grope thru my surrender
for some bit of juju
to hold us here, now

just like this

MOANIN' GROANIN' BLUES

when i get up in the mornin'
know i've lived to see another day
when i get up with cockcrow
know i've lived to see another day
if my dreary weren't so goddamned weary
i wouldn't carry on this way

get up in the mornin'
gotta face another sun
get up in the mornin'
gotta face another sun
i'm so sick and tired of slavin'
hard work and trouble nevah have no fun

goin' back down in my blanket
put my misery to the wall
gonna dive down in my blanket
turn my broke face to the wall
ain't nothin' gonna rouse me
till i hear the trumpet call

refrain: what's life if all you know
             of life is pain
             what's life if all you know
             of life is pain
             what's the good in sufferin'
             if ain't no good to gain

when i get up in the mornin'
know i've made it thru another night
when i get up in the mornin'

194

i know i've made it thru another night
mister gloom doom come to get me
still weak yet strong enough to fight

AMERICAN SONNET (8)

not just another marketeer

a billion a year racket owned by
everyday business folk
an exciting all-cash opportunity
the latest schemology! no monthly overhead!
run it at home or out of the trunk of your car
can be operated part-time earning you deep
pockets while you keep your regular job
no experience or special training needed
start today with low initial investment

quick returns/the coins stack up
your latest crack at securing a future

try it yourself. it's high-octane for
maintaining cool under pressure

AMERICAN SONNET (9)

love people use things

later a possible emergence as
effortless forms of illumination drift
across the screen of the set/swaying bodies
converging/ghosts of divisions
city after city. oh ruthless decay
—these skin disruptions—
the sport of confession for pay
(loose shoes, tight pussy, warm place to shit)
splendid moments when all visions of ghosts/
convergences/bodies swaying adrift
illuminating new behavioral norms
effortless emergence? possibly. later

use people love things

send all dispatches
in tongue
swallow blue notes whole

MESSAGE FROM XANADU (2)

never use your spirit name
you want to be able to get a decent gig
and will be deferred mysteriously
without adequate explanation or redress

you will need a bogus passport, visa and stolen
currency to cross the border of equanimity
they will start rumors and your
friends will discover aspects of you
which were suspected but which they did not
want to know

they will bug your toilet and even your shit
will betray you

they will fix your brakes so your mind
won't be able to stop when you hit
a dangerous curve

they will have you assassinated by pianos

AMERICAN SONNET (10)

after Lowell

our mothers wrung hell and hardtack from row
    and boll. fenced others'
gardens with bones of lovers. embarking
    from Africa in chains
reluctant pilgrims stolen by Jehovah's light
    planted here the bitter
seed of blight and here eternal torches mark
    the shame of Moloch's mansions
built in slavery's name. our hungered eyes
    do see/refuse the dark
illuminate the blood-soaked steps of each
    historic gain. a yearning
yearning to avenge the raping of the womb
    from which we spring

AMERICAN SONNET (11)

the moon is livid white. pacifica boils
we are going under
ship afire the sea pools with blood

women and children first

i cannot swim
and i have been refused a mae west

i fight the mob to board a lifeboat
a bronze-haired aryan roughly grabs me by my arm
his eyes a feast of loathing
a tear tattooed beneath his left orb

"i have as much right to live as anyone"
i demand. he slams me to the deck

"go back to the jungle where you belong"
he spits. "and stay there"

NOISE (2)

sanctimonious cacophonifiers ricochet on stucco
fill the gap between wish and want

nose to nose
the delicious quadrasonic of thigh slapping thigh

if you keep the tv on and the stereo at the same time
you can erase space

blues ooze/the trumpeting simulcast cum

he eats all my silences

AYIN OR NO ONE

wind or voice of god?

the well-traveled road out of eden turns upon itself oases
layers of elaborate multicolored sheets the way flesh dampens
and gives burst to salt in excessive heats dilated eyes roll up
and inward to whiten to circumscribe their own final shutter-
ings windows boarded up nailed against intrusive harsh abusive
sun against dust from unpaved roads snaking unwinding across
three thousand miles of concrete majesty and fifty-odd years of
thrashings up the amazon of the soul to her narrow darkened
pathway jungled-down and threatening where she waits
breathing deeply air of hunger vamp-shaman jihad-monger
mother-of-the-city maker-of-roads her emotive tar sticky in the
siroccan blaze captures the imprint of his eagerness his steps
this traveler (fleeing holocaust) he's come in exploration/hadj
the metropolis this ageless romance a shanker a miracle cause
for shame cause for glory such fevers such contraindications/
neuroses

"is the glass half full or half empty?" he asked.
"it depends on how thirsty i am," she answered.

the road ever onward the traveler naked and blind (nakedly
blind) in lust an elongation that stiffens with satori drums drum-
ming intensifies the act an unwinding turning in into her
pomegranate eyes her raven mouth the cave of the giver crypt
of the taker her holy hole thru which he simooms pain endur-
ing forced labor the by-product of their night's cabal the child-
stuff suctioned from her womb into a necrotic blackness ever

202

stillborn harmony the abortion/disembowelment of song frustrated/choked by the twisted umbilicus of hate his hardness the stubborn thrusts which storm her eyes flood her backwater dirt roads to spiritual el dorados the greedy claw of anger mauling her slave's heart as abusive as that urban sun endless poverty her eyes closed in wonder/submission to his davening the savour of his red sweat stinging her bluesy lips his hazel eyes relentless harmattans (he mounts he enters he descends) as on sheets twisted back on butt-weary mattresses stinking of generations of excessive demands tongue and again tongue their frictions one traveling flesh of the other over and over this ritual coitus/ rendering of

delirium

POETRY LESSON NUMBER THREE

solikeman have you read this cat's stuff
like he's a believer man, dig, you should really
hear this

and he shuffles the papers at me, Paul does
with deep admiration, kicks back and renders me
speechless, his gray eyes tearing. the words sing
of bird holiday dolphy

solikeman, this cat is legend should be as famous
as anybody. was there at the beginning. like when
The Beat Thing was really happenin'. he believes
in The Muse, man, he *believes*

what's that? i ask

what's what?

what is The Muse?

likeGreekman, Erato, the godwomanlover of lyrical
verse, man. dig, you should *meet* this guy. he's pure
and bring some of your stuff. the cat is beautiful
you'll see

so we go west to Venice for the hang. we find him
in the back of the big space filled with empty
folding chairs and a handful of acolytes rattling
around the mike. Paul slobbers all over himself making
with the intros. the man is frail, bent, not as old as he
looks, ill and perhaps dying (i've heard). his long salt but
mainly pepper hair tied back in a long slim ponytail, white
hands trembling. Paul emotes something recently written

what'd you think man. what'd you think?

the beautiful cat leans into his cane with one hand,
holds out the other

let me see it.

he takes the poem and reads it closely, smiles, returns it

not bad. keep at it, Paul.

she's a poet too, man, like amateur, but she's
trying, dig? can you look at one of her pieces
justaminute ifyoudon'tmind? she's got it right here

i go into my purse and shyly hand him a couple of
pages. he reads them and smiles. word eyes glitter

you've got something.

but she needs work, doesn't she man? Paul says
doesn't she need work?

find your mentors, young lady. all great poets have
had their mentors

we go outside and stroll the boardwalk in
contemplation. Paul is restless and upset

did you hear what the cat said to you back there
did you hear that?

hear what?

he liked your shit, man. he really dug your
shit, man. i know the cat. he never talks to me like that

like what?

he said you've got something

come on, are you jealous?

hell no, man. i just wish he'd respond to me the
way he responds to you

forget it, Paul. besides, i don't believe all
that muse stuff anyway. it's a lot of hooey

nomanno! how can you say something like that? The
Muse is for real. i know. and it's so goddamn hard
to create without her. you know what i mean. like
inspiration. like from above

he took an exaggerated look skyward

it's just that if i waited around for some muse
i wouldn't get much done

i don't know about you, man, idon'tknowaboutchew
you shouldn't say things like that

huh?

that's sacrilege, man. *sacrilege*

i don't tell him i don't know the meaning of the
word. when we get home later we make love and
afterwards i go and look it up in the unabridged
while he's snoring

MOON LAYING ON HER SIDE

value is as value does

i can't get good service or is it just me?
i use my real name
but the best i can do is imagine small's paradise
who do i thank for being so skunked
so razzed so out of sync

excuse me for the eyes in the back of my head

sad

of thee of thee of thee singing
i am bold patriot. i embrace the nation/notion
that condemns me. i've never confessed
to anything that wasn't public policy. all i
ever wanted was enuff green to cover the black

i cook all day i cook all night
i conjure conjure till the roux is right

(he says i have a high mind
and a whore's hips)

i prepare the oven
for a meal of bones
for a plate of the lover
who leaves me alone

when social dally becomes habit — arf arf
rewriting the turf as i rave thru it

stripped naked

my truth hangs by its nappy mane
strung up in the candy shop window
its hands crossed over its pubis, sprays

the third element of creation

AFTERWARDS WE MAKE UP

blood among my tears

this is our room full of eyes opinions angers
we write out our texts here
i wear nylon he goes nude

volumes of ill-stacked books threaten to fall
brown terry cloth bath towels hug doorknobs
jazz aria or treatise/running lines define
our issues/marital strategy (status post altercation)

the quilt a scripted passion. a ruthless shimmy
recovery uncertain. broken glass

our communication is punctuated by violence
the willful grammar of artistic insecurity
too many commas too many
exclamation points

ethnocentric juxta/my pink-brown labia quakes
under the assault of his obsessive semitic tongue

as his philosophical disposition hardens
(synergism abandoned for more
solipsistic venues)

my body his again

POST-MODERN POUNDING

i am tired of trafficking the long sizzling grid
that names this city names me

born late born wrong

bopbopshebang

a whitmanesque stroke between
shadow and space—alone but not lonesome

is what's required
to be taken by the illusion of escape/fooled
however brief

but seriously

(little mother. let me tell you about men. how men
love other men. how a woman is a means to give
a man back to himself. how she is measured)

speaking of fox holes and fast lanes
of passages and schemes

the zip zap zooey

tired of pain and complaints of pain

i beat my head. i beat my head

VIOLENCES

cruel rumors of a wealth never achieved
causing unearned winkings of eyes

the awful need in the eyes of the boy in
the yellowed mirror of his mother

hawk eyes of the boys roving up the
minor's cutoffs all in his pockets

she bites down into it then spits out
an eye

the whipping cord her eyes inflamed the
whipping cord her "gotcha"

boy-eyes stone-hard and sharp draw
blood to her skin's mahogany surface

capsized she near-drowns in an ocean of eyes

coming like headlights she's struck down
his startled eyes drive over her

the eyes of the dancing boy out on the
floor jitter like irreverent beads

later they find her dangling. at her neck
the rope of eyes

ESSAY ON LANGUAGE (4)

the question of meaning always arises
i have been charged with setting
my sights too low

when there's no way to come away
satisfied

what lady bluesed about

the assassin of english is for hire
he can't get it wholesale anymore
he can't get it period—the hedonistic
failure to repeat early poetic success

not enough cookies
to make it worth his rhyme

the meaning of love is always in the next embrace

(what the snake doctor does
down to the root—a cure)

extrasensory persuasion
after i eat him up i lick the brains

ugly is skin deep
but ignorance is to the bone

Part 4: The laying on of. . . .

CREATURE OF TWO WORLDS

not gravity. the weight of worry
holds me to earth

lately i am a dweller under music with antennae
and gills. i move with the obscene certainty
of instinct. with the rolling joyful glide of
sultry rhythms. a new form venturing
among coral

it is the swamp that feeds me. the bittersweet
things i find on the underside that scuttle
on the surface, wade helplessly in my path
grow without sun, thriving on the
vulcanic radiance of meaning

not gravity. the weight of my desire
holds me to him

as we meet/the genetically programmed mating of
different species/a secret race which peoples
the devonian doom of a subterranean past.
i am impregnated
with the memory of his longing

a weakened seed gains strength in my blood
takes root in my word as i crawl toward shore
and give birth

not gravity. the weight of ancestral pain
holds me to strive

to break free of a murky history to leap beyond
its fictions/brave the treacherous currents of

melancholy straits. propelled by blind
devotion i swim toward the unknowable

not gravity. love
weights me to earth

BIRD EVIDENCE

she-swan on water. above a honking. the unkind
reflection defies all ripples. she remains untransformed.
no grand plumage stunted wings cheat her of extended
flight. she is embroiled and overstuffed

the cat has her in its paw. big soft paw curiously
explores her frantic flutter. to get away. to get away.
she offers meager chirps to the bird-god. to be
set free or swallowed whole

make a sound. name it. seafood

speckled, well-trussed, succulent she is presented
for the feast. carved. served. each bite of her enters
them. peahen down to their marrow. suck the bones
a delicious victory

flitters off-shore in the slick of civil spill
feathers gummy with a tenacious abstraction/
a second skin. this belligerent thoughtless
intelligence rids the world of her flock

as rare as the pink pelican

THE STONE CAT

it needs no wicker
no one feeds it. it needs no one

the stone cat is poised at the edge of a succulent bush
it is the color of dried pink rose petals

it can be caressed. gives back
no caresses

flesh is too messy. makes too many demands

lifelessness lends superiority
a specific kind of liberation

imaginary stone cat purrs at strokes of rain

the stone cat. lovely in its
private rigor

the sun on its back. the sun

SUDDEN VACANCY

i sit and stare at the room

my hope used to bunk there. and my joy too. and
everything i thought good. my faith. my continuance.
my other self. myself in selves. my laughter also had a
corner of that room. small little space it held so much—
the enormity of my thriving/beauty kept selfishly
secret from all but a few

now. oh how empty, room.

a tortured gap. my desires removed/old useless
furniture. greedy hands have left their prints in the
dust and on the walls

(did i have all that. did i smile. did i feel safe?
did i admire leaves of bougainvillea growing at the window
did i lose the onus of skin in a scent of fame. did i move
with grace in his arms. did i share a sweet sorrow with
her. did i dance before an audience of lovers?)

i did a cradle crow
i did a hush-a-bye

did and i did woo night favors and seduced an ode

the room. too still. its music
stilled. there are bits and pieces of melodrama
left clinging in the filthy orange rug

mildew denial and lies

DEATH DON'T DRINK WATER

death don't like warm hands
don't care much for green plants speckled in
white sitting in little pots soaking up sun
shake rattle and roll is one of its favorite songs
death never learned the 2-step but can sure enuff
shimmy stomp bump-and-grind much ass and always leads
death don't need reefer to get high. ain't into
candy and has a peculiar sweetness all its own

JUST BEFORE GEORGE RISES

fever consumes him

he can't walk even with a walker
the days move thru him
as does light
and the only place he walks
is where i remember him

like the time i backed up the car
a few inches each time he reached the door
so he couldn't get in
because the handle eluded his grasp
a joke
and i laughed and laughed as he admonished
his impish daughter

and now he's barely able to breathe
as i sit and watch and beg him
let go let go Pop. it is time to let go
yet he clings. his grip still strong
even tho his breath is shallow
he clings to the bed as if

he can't speak except to
make raspy uh-huhs. this tells us
he's still partly of this world if mainly
of the other. his eyes focus on us
at times to let us know he still sees what's
going on. he sees his great grandson
the one who is rose red but who has inherited
his nose

and it hurts to swallow water
even a drop of water

and here we sit as if the weight of our
bodies cleaves him to earth

here we sit in his final hours
suspended

BEDTIME STORY

bed calls. i sit in the dark in the living room
trying to ignore them

in the morning, especially Sunday mornings
it will not let me up. you must sleep
longer, it says

facing south
the bed makes me lay heavenward on my back
while i prefer a westerly fetal position
facing the wall

the bed sucks me sideways into it when i
sit down on it to put on my shoes. this
persistence on its part forces me to dress in
the bathroom where things are less subversive

the bed lumps up in anger springs popping out to
scratch my dusky thighs

my little office sits in the alcove adjacent to
the bed. it makes strange little sighs
which distract me from my work
sadistically i pull back the covers
put my typewriter on the sheet and turn it on

the bed complains that i'm difficult duty
its slats are collapsing. it bitches when i
blanket it with books and papers. it tells me
it's made for blood and bone

lately spiders ants and roaches
have invaded it searching for food

GHOST OF A DANCE

it was one of those moments when she wanted
to be alone with her past

rarely had she felt the power of her new-found beauty, but
she was at her trimmest, elegantly tall and young enough
to enjoy the floor-length powder blue crepe gown accented in
blue velvet, how it gloved her body. she wore nothing under-
neath save a push-up bra and a scent called afrodesia. close
observation might betray the vague impression of her kinky
bush at the crown of her long maple legs.

she didn't expect to meet anyone she knew, but he was there

he was very tall, tawny-skinned, heavy-set, clean-cut. she
recognized her old classmate. those were burr-headed pain-
filled high-school days when she was ugliest girl on campus
chosen most likely to stop a clock or turn a poor boy to
stone. she had spent her prom night ironing the family wash
in front of the television.

those hate-filled voices from adolescence vanished as the
jazz orchestra struck up a blues waltz and he crossed the
room, held out an arm and asked her to dance. she looked
into his eyes. they welcomed her. she accepted and went into
his embrace. they moved in flawless rhythm spinning out
and across the floor, swirling the way she had always
imagined it would be if

as their dance ended she grew afraid to look at him
and afraid to speak. teary-eyed she dashed from his arms,
to the door, down a flight of stairs, into the night, never

224

looking back. she had experienced all the perfection
she had ever wanted

it was more than she could stand

CANCER

1

the jagged cutting of skin

        (out. cut all the black out)

death the air we breathe death the food we eat
unnatural chemical transfixion/invisibility kills

diseased/corrupted

X marks the social topograph

i place the gluttonous dead in the inactive file

2

the married man refuses to propagate. his wife wants his
        child
born inside her. they are stoic lives/shaped sacrifice. *it
is the family curse,* he whispers. it truncates and sometimes
aborts happiness. he's doomed. the blood legacy — it will —
the lungs — it will — the prostate — it will — the stomach

it will
he bears it but no child of his ever

3

the life technologist ponders mortification/significant
        unknowns

        daddy-so-independent before they cut the bad out
        you in your cap of scars

226

your hair grows back but you are not the same
it is excised but there are seizures
it is excised but there is fear
it is excised but you are reduced

old yes helplessly old

4

chronic human ailing

doctors move thru well-lit halls in fresh white starched
   smocks
tired professional patience ruts foreheads
circles eyes

 remission
 remission
 remission

chronic human failing

swelling. diarrhea. vertigo
lenticular opacities

nocturnal bleeding. sweats. yellow sputum
shadows cling to skin

 remit. remit
 please remit
 amount due is indicated

urogenital pain/rectal carcinoma. surgery

(out. carve it all out)

"the mind is a powerful thing," says the healer, "you must
    believe"

5

there is something on my face
it has a life of its own. it grows. it can't
come off. at night it sleeps
i toss restless, worried. there is nothing
medical science can do

6

unchecked metastases

pain in the neck/carcinoma of the esophagus

— cobalt —

(out. burn it all out)

pus in the urine. a deficit in erythrocytes. i'm screaming
under the microscope. prognosis terminal

ecoleukemia

— numentherapy —

(out. baptize it all out)

some jitterbug. some tango. some slow-dance

7

mama long hours lengthen mama hospital bills loom
and threaten mama the big fear bigger mama the

grave looms, threatens mama your voice a shriek mama
don't panic mama ask questions

doctors are not gods

8

there is something in my heart
it has a reality of its own
it grows
won't come out
at night it wakes
i toss in restless sleep

there is nothing metaphysical science can do

9

the room stinks of black stool. the body tortured shrunken
there a pan to vomit in. there the life support unit
its solitary bleeps denote life. tight smiling nurses
in severe white ease in and out to decipher temperature
        blood pressure pulse

aching anxious eyes of loved ones search for movement
a flutter a flit and find love unresponsive
leave

a silent prayer

                you get some rest now

MY DADDY BE A BABY

he sits propped up in the giant crib
while my mama feed him

my daddy be a baby
he wears diapers that must be changed

my daddy be a baby he lay curl up
on his side in dark night

my daddy be a baby my turn to
rock him in my arms tell him
it's gonna be all right

my turn to lullaby

my daddy be a baby he cry
for his mama long crossed over
tell her he comin' at last

GEORGE DEATH ANNIVERSARY

papa do you hear the grass grow?

do you talk rainbow

papa do you feel earth tremor
on its axis?

what kind of jazz do the planets blow?

can you knot one end of time
to the other?

can you navigate the doubt between
hope and despair?

in which universe is justice found?

how much laughter will it take
to fill your absence?

OF AN ABSENCE

his silence would've been manna. just to be together enuff.
he could sit and read a book or write or correct papers or
read the sports page, giving her stats on the playoffs. and now
and again looking up to see if she's holding up. or standing
beside her at the window looking out and below. it would be
nice to speak in soft concerned nothings rife with mutual
understanding. this difficult time for her made less difficult
by his sacrifice. to be near. she might hold his hand for
a second. or he might tell her there's something in the corner
of her eye. or smile to himself and remind her of time
precious time. he might kiss her to express his love and
irritate her skin with his beard. they could go down to the
cafeteria for her coffee and his tea. then return later to see
how things have gone

MY ENLARGED HEART

an avaricious eater of oxygen
there is barely room for the chambered cry
itself beating against me
it threatens arrest

the doctor enters his blackness robed
in sterile white

       "your heart is enlarged, twice normal"

my face toward the examination room wall
cold kiss of his stethoscope against my back

       "you need a change a rest less stress
       take off twenty pounds
       stop salt butter marijuana"

he asks me to cough. i bark in the
space of a single beat

pain on gasping. pump harder. not knowing
pump harder. until the surge breaks. pump harder
longer

       "you worry too much about this world"

quick gulps for air. i breathe deep, sigh
the pulse provides motive

       (social denial a lack of recognition
       fear that i'm truly inferior
       a greedy lover children for whom
       i am inadequate provider compulsive

eating a disdain for exercise fear of
death before fulfillment)

from right to left
my flow of blood is uncontrolled

wild palpitations

MacHOSPITAL

the child screams. screams for mother. screams
for God. screams "don't." screams "it
hurts." screams and screams for daddy

a break. a silence

then it comes again. the screaming

getting off the elevator i see them. everyone who
works here has to see them, there's no evasion
no place to hide from it. no employees'
hang. this charity facility was established
around the start of the century. i hear some old rich
white dowager keeps it in blood money. the building
i work in is named for her. recently, a popular
fast food chain has become a major contributor

there's an institutional motto: "we care." and we do

the turnover is a bitch. by the time you've learned
a new employee's name, they're gone. the hardnosed
the hard-up and the dedicated stay, faces of
smiling stone—black white hispanic, a few asians—
we blacks hang in longest. that thang in our history
prepares us for on-going pain and suffering. those
with good pension plans die in the saddle. i rank
among the hard-up

this is a cold-blooded place, caring limited to
the children for whom we care. no one has time or budget
to sympathize with adults. we know
how absolutely lucky adults are to be adult

many of these kids will never make it

you see them yet you don't see them. it's understood
you don't register shock. the shocked go into a
restroom lock the door and cry. the shocked
may be fired within a relatively short time for showing
shock. the shocked are hasty to seek work elsewhere. the
shocked get the hell out one way or another

my face that smiles that's also stone

holding elevator doors open for women wrestling
with strollers wheelchairs gurneys is utmost courtesy
the men have left them eighty-five percent of fathers
of disabled children leave mom to tough it out
alone. (it ain't his fault the baby was imperfect. who
did the drug. who had the bad gene pool. who fucked
around. who God cursed. who who who. i, said the
sparrow with my little bow and arrow)

mom may be no saint. there are foster homes and
institutes. bureaucratic warehousing

the kids hurt. seeing kids hurt i hurt. i learn
to turn it off

there was the darlin' five-year-old son of
the rock stars. they came in dressed for fame, tall
thin in fashion in jewelry in attitude—baaad
beautiful young black dutiful—and stood in the hallways
for hours, too old a story: the kid with natural charm
the kid who seduces everyone with his preciousness
innocence freshness. name it

when his hair began to thin i realized
it was falling out. some days

he was listless and milky about his skin
and some days gloom displaced fame
on those sweet glamorous faces (war. what
true war is about)

i stop myself and turn it off. i can't let myself
feel for their child

"this is a job," my maxim

i ride the elevator my smile of stone intact
eyes sensitized to the smallness, ready for the
too real bugged eyes of down's syndrome the cranial
distortions of hydrocephaly the twisted limbs of
accidents the visual evidence of the chromosomal
damages of one drug or another—the "premees" the
spinal deformities—the monsters

businesses and a few music tv stars donate
time toys money. there's a biannual telethon. a resident
artist practices healing thru self expression

the first artist i met was a black man, quite
excellent himself. it was interesting to see what
he extracted from the children. bright vivid stark
masterpieces hung outside the cafeteria. i'd stop and
admire images of death frustration the Devil hope—
even exciting bold abstracts—work good enough for the
galleries. he left. a younger white woman took over
suddenly butterflies buttercups dolls and birdies—
pastels appeared

it's true what they say, i thought, *children are a canvas*
i avoided artists after that

yes. the sights disturb me. disrupt my sleep
a nightmare my daughter's hair thinned to her scalp
symptomatic of a brain tumor/chemotherapy
what can i do? i can't let my child die without
a fight. i sit straight up in bed
shocked into jittering clarity

i handle the screams with my walkman kept in
the upper right-hand drawer of my desk which
effectively mutes the cries for God for father for
mother for the doctor to stop hurting
for the hurting to stop

they're to be seen everywhere, the child population
mixed in with professional and ancillary adults

it is stunningly profound
how important
a piece of paper
may be to little sick and dying
bits of humanity

all colors shames and sizes

some of these kids won't make it, i think as i
watch them exit elevators on crutches struggling to
walk. mobility is life. the limbs grow frail. sores
appear at the neck. limbs are lost. something fungal —
a rash related to immuno-deficiency. a malformation
of head face palate

i watch them my eyes bleed
as i pass on the way to photocopy on my way to
lunch on my way home to my hard life waiting
to my children. and if one chances to look my way

i've got my stone smile ready
they're precious, all of them, is how i look at it —

service

GONE BUT NOT FORGOTTEN

gone real gone the good die gone

strange and distant banging wakes me from reverie
my bed is cold. i am cold but deep long sleep
is good for me

it's time for song when going gets gone

i hear voices sing and shout, hear bodies
move anxiously about. i hear the
diggings of an eager race for whom i've
disappeared without a trace

grieving of the gone goes on and on

and now they've rediscovered me. want to make use
of me. overturn all my stones. make a science
of my bones. my past once ignored in ignominy, they
now wish a future built on me

there is no such thing as coming back

such a strange sensation — the living
at my grave dying to get in

WHAT THE WALLS SAY

he spends too much time
in the bathroom

you know him not but he knows you. his eyes
mirror only what you see in yourself. behind
them is nothing

he eats hardy
but always looks unhealthy

he devours children as he was devoured by
his mother. know him by the stealth with
which he appears and disappears

there is something dirty he
can't make clean. take care. he
will infect you

he gives off the chalky dung of fear. keep your
floors clear of it. watch each step. he will
strike right before your eyes

he has a supernatural sense of
smell. he always knows when
you're guessing

protect yourself and your children. burn all
passages to your heart

he will tempt you to murder. resist. to kill him
is to never be rid of him

UNFINISHED GHOST STORY (3)

he woke in two shakes in a sweat and sat up in bed. she was staring at him. her eyes had a peculiar glow. he asked what was wrong. she told him she was a sleepwalker but since she was sitting mid-floor in a lotus he knew this was a lie but said nothing

one afternoon he came home unexpectedly and discovered her nude in the bedroom on all fours eating something from a round dish. she didn't hear him so he tiptoed out, went to a neighborhood bar, had a few beers, then came home again making sure to cause a stir

on Saturday he was rummaging around for the lost mate to one of his socks when he spotted a fuzzy little gray feather poked out of her dresser drawer. he opened it and found a green and yellow feather cresting a neatly folded pile of her nylon slips. he lifted them carefully to discover a shallow box containing an assortment of small dead birds. quickly he replaced the slips and closed the drawer

when he noticed the diary at the bottom of the nightstand on her side of the bed, he opened it. all the pages were blank. but between several of them were wedged oddly shaped swatches of cloth and various locks of strange hair

lately, when fucking, she's begun taking small bites of his ears, neck, chest, shoulders, upper arms bordering on serious pain nevertheless transfixing him, intensifying his orgasms to the extent he feels exhausted even after a full night's sleep

when she threw away all his white cotton shirts he knew it was time to bury the past

UNFINISHED GHOST STORY (4)

he's new she's new they're news together
a universe composed of two revitalized spirits
they waft up the avenue spinning in private orbit
one around the other mutually rapt they fail to
see her estranged poltergeist parked curbside
he barks a harsh hello. they turn and stare at the
shimmering mass of heat and anger coming towards them
"who is this guy," the poltergeist demands. she
senses trouble and to avoid it asks her new encounter
to go on ahead while she straightens things. he
cooperates reluctantly after a kiss

"what's this all about?" her ex-poltergeist trembles. she
feels sorry for it. it was once the major spook in
her ethnosphere

"what'd you expect? you left me. i have my needs. i
don't like being alone."

"what can he do that i can't?"

"that's not the point. i care about tomorrow. with
him it's possible."

"what about me?"

"go back to your mother. we'll commune later."

he shook/a snit of rage and hot emanations then
disappeared in a huff of auto exhaust

the ill-digested keeps coming up, she thought. when i
get home i'm gonna have to purge my crystal ball

UNFINISHED GHOST STORY (5)

it is the eve of the eclipse. jupiter is setting altho venus
still gleams brightly in the west. mars can be seen best at
full sunset. it rained on this July day for the first time in
recorded history. a number of large imposing spiders inhabit
the corners of the kitchen bathroom and master bedroom.
a mysterious white powder is laid down in certain places. the
flame from a blue scented candle glimmers atop the dresser.
numerous books and manuscripts nest on dust-flecked shelves.
muffled she-cries can be heard faintly emanating from the
        walls.

something fiercely bangs against the gated front door
to get in

UNFINISHED GHOST STORY (6)

Sydney was alone in their bedroom crying over her difficulties when she heard the noise. she stopped and listened. there was a distinct rustling sound. she reached for the box of scented tissues on the mahogany bedside table, snatched up two and gently dabbed her reddened eyes. if it was Caldwell coming in she didn't want him to catch her in such an unpleasant state. he despised weak women and so she did her best to keep her failings to herself. again the odd rustling sound interrupted her worries

"Caldwell?" she called out. there was no answer

she slipped on her green silk robe and went downstairs to investigate. as she came to the dark kitchen she noted a dim light. the door of the refrigerator had somehow come open. as she reached to close it she was assaulted by a large leafy ice-cold head of crisp romaine lettuce

PRISONER OF LOS ANGELES (3)

bars of black flesh on celluloid
a glitter palace structured of purple rage
day upon day upon daze
blues calendar of grand miseries
barely subsisting on a diet of false hope
(shit over shingles)
i bleed stars
sentenced for refusing to spill the dreams
how long before the anthem of my pulse
slows to a gasping red whine
how long before i'm starved into betrayal
hang by my own want
who is the keeper of the key
what god has locked me to this land
for failure to believe

PRUNE SPOON JUNE

this peculiar summer we stroll the boardwalk
on Venice Beach/a year-round circus
boutiques have displaced dwellings
muscles mentors

i try not to wear your skin. i try not to
mimic your walk. i try hard not to scheme
as hard as you. i try not to bring her little
gifts the way you used to. i try not to miss you

we come upon the ebony dwarf who jerks his
full-sized hips to funky disco his contempt
for the normal in height as bodacious as
shocking as the charcoal carrot-shaped stubs
he mercilessly flaps to the rhythm
daring passersby to throw dollars or
any change to be spared

(lost mother searches for children)

the sightless seer admires bikinis. praises the
tenacity of sand and body fat. blows for pizza

platinum-blue horizon inches away

browsing thru old postcards, i find one fit for
an ex-friend who died of the virus

no time to visit your grave
too busy fighting to stay out of mine

AFTER THE POEM (3)

the reading is over. satisfied/it was
good we go out to relax with her and her
new boyfriend. we order chardonnay
he puts in for a beer
                        when she gets up
to go to the jane he begins to nervously
toy with the little vase sitting mid-table
posing a fat stiff-stemmed
                        amber grunge.
"perhaps he's not used to being around someone
Black," i think. then decide, no. it's a
class thang. he's probably self-conscious
because he's the only one in the group who's
not a poet
                without warning he lifts the vase
snaps off the head of the mothy bloom
with his teeth. chews and swallows it
then grins at me, ear-to-ear
having made his point

DREAM 2610

the professor is explaining the
comparative nature of the fossil before us in
lab. plant life and human bone. how the layerings
of time affect structure

i've never seen her before

the wild-eyed high-yellow woman in white
crepe dress with tracks of black pin-stripes
loosely belted at her waist and flapping madly
as she comes racing down the hallway, brunet
hair hard-pressed against her scalp, a rubberband
defining her ponytail and she's moving so fast it's
straight-out behind her as she dashes into the
room brandishing the hypodermic

knocking the table and fossil helter-skelter,
she jabs me in the arm with it, releasing
some of the substance

then she

hot-pops herself and starts to spazz. i go
into shocked rage/feel my system fighting a
mounting wooziness

her eyes roll back in her head as she goes
down the professor trying to help her/save her
life others rushing to our aid hands grabbing at me
as i look for something/find my shoe its rubbery
thick blackness and take the shoe and start slapping
the woman upside her head even as she slips into coma

screaming "don't suicide on me bitch!
don't suicide on me! goddamn it don't die
before i can kill you"

why are you so upset, something says, *it's only a dream*

abruptly i wake
lay there staring up into the indigo
calming my heart a full five
minutes before the alarm starts
bleeding in my ear

IMITATION OF DEATH

here sit i at the womb of my desire here
sit i my fingers slowly sweep across
chiseled indentations

spell my name

black head of stone rising from a bed of dreams

pronounce my name

no wind and no sun. fingers rivering eyes
devoid of fears. here sit i

oooh the trouble seen

grave task of staying still. waiting for an
imagined past to reveal some secret. or
important breath-making formula

uncover my name

loam soaking in skeleton. mold foxing in
the world. time silencing rancor
hands scraping the entombing dark

leave no name

only

the hollow husk of a former dweller
underground filled with inquisitive plaster
at the site of excavation. hauled skyward

to be resentenced

DREAM 1319

i am in my father's house

it is made entirely of fine cedar, unfurnished
the floors fairly clean but in corners
dust and bits of stuff indicate
premises vacated mere hours before

i go upstairs to the second floor and stand
mid-room. it is large with high ceiling
suddenly i see a movement

something rolls or crawls across the floor
set in a golden glow

at first look it is a scarab. no. a gold coin

i go down on hands and knees. closer it is one of
Pop's old roller erasers the kind mounted on a miniature
whisk to brush away the tiny pilings. it's gold instead of
the gray i remember as a child. even the dried
rubber cement which cakes it is gold

but as it rolls
the pilings form a giant cursive "G" then
it rolls towards me. and with it comes a cold
i let the cold come over me expecting it to pass
but it lingers and the eraser spins mid-floor as
i feel myself taken into extreme cold bone cold then
deeper. and i know

and i tell myself smartly
"you'd better wake up"

i do so at once

this too an illusion

here on earth such choice hells

the way i see it the way i smell it
the way it tastes. how it feels vis-a-vis newsprint

lately i've noticed i frighten blonde children when they
come upon me unexpected. the embarrassed parent grabs
        the child
irked that such an issue should disturb
a leisurely afternoon's shop

(baby it's you at my heart you with electrodes transistors
and silicone chips you with that code blue quark

you counting the rads around my nuclear bomb site)

happiness relative to roach-butt and time to burn

juke me
juke me
juke me till we come music

you can never tell can never tell how never tell how sweet
        tell how
sweet how sweet a woman is sweet a woman is
by how she looks

lately i am given to speaking in tongues and
long inland lapses

THE UMBRELLAS OF TEJON-LEBEC

many look few see

mama called at six o'clock the morning time changed. while half
asleep she'd heard via broadcast that one of the damned things
had broken loose and slain a sightseer. they're closing down the
exhibit. did we still want to go? after all, it's just a talk radio
rumor of killer umbrellas. we opt to make our decision en route

news reports verify the rumor. on death's intrusion the twenty-
odd-million dollar indulgence is ordered closed by its stunned
creator three days ahead of schedule. in Japan as in California.
mama wants to see it more than ever, even if most of the seven-
teen hundred "monstrosities" are shut down. we agree we want
to someday tell our grandchildren we saw Christo's Folly. it's
well worth braving bad weather and worse traffic even if we're
late too late for full hillside bloom

a thirty-three-year-old mother was smashed into the rocks. hours
later a Japanese crane operator is electrocuted while dismantling
the blue umbrellas. my lover and i debate the timing/morali-
ty/wisdom of such art. thousands of citizens are homeless. too
many of those stricken by the virus can't get treatment or
decent digs in which to die

meanwhile

majestic iridescent yellow parasols rise out of moist gray mist
mountainward: some lowered and tightly bound flapping against
the wind, giant stubborn maize ghosts. a few storm-battered

256

by gusts of sixty-five miles per hour have become fiery gold monarchs poised skyward. others are husks of starfish splat against earth. some lay lop-sided crashed over on tilted five-hundred pound cement anchors. one snapped free and skittered amok along the northbound lanes of the interstate. others, mere emaciated flaggings

on this road less taken the sign reads
closed ahead

THE EDGE OF DAWN

he checks in at midnight to complete his peace. thoughts and feelings are chaotic; an unspeakable loathing, remorse, rage which alternate with numbness, blistering shame and an odd serenity nearing bliss.

his young taut muscular frame speaks of love of the gym and working out. he fills the cramped, musty, aged hotel corridor. the tiny room borders on clean and is as drab as imagined; single bed with thin sheets, brass fixtures tinged with green, light bulb sans shade casting an uncomfortable glare over the dinginess. the bathroom is a closet; basin of chipped enamel, stool stinking of a multitude of overloads, shower of cement and tile with heavy brown plastic drape concealing a stainless steel nozzle.

there's a mirror in a cream-colored frame poised over the basin. in it he tallies stolen years. it throws back his mahogany skin and close-cut nappy hair. negro but nevertheless good-looking. that was the discount. he hasn't had his chance. if he'd had the money he'd be at the Hilton instead.

there's no air conditioning. a tightly screened window faces the street two stories below. he opens it and soaks in the hustling sounds of despair: distant shrieks of sirens, the muted fhupp-fhupp of police copter blades, the lyrical hyperchatter of needle freaks, crack dealers and winos who prowl this turf punctuated by the periodic squeal of brakes as someone curbs to score. this is Hollywood in throes. his choice. to break clean; become evident. no fear and no pity. there are too many begging for understanding; too many doing talk-show interviews; too many swamping charities in pursuit of dignity.

he anticipates discovery: she'll enter his room with her

passkey; a middle-aged, heavyset "sistuh" in work gloves, dungarees and sneakers; she won't cry out because life has, at last, inured her to shock. her heart will embrace him as if he were her own. she'll blow her labored breath and descend three flights of stairs to the front desk. she'll tell what she's seen. then she'll go on to complete her shift.

the investigation will be brief.

no identification. one young black male, approximately twenty-years old, depressed, good guess that he had the virus. cut his own throat. kkkkrist whatta mess. looka this he left a note. unfuckin' believable.

what's it say?

two words: pardon me.

THE MOTH

brushing up against his bearded cheek

hope nursed on fear genocide at random
winging against desert wind the making of exaggerated
spirals cold promise of how to live evermore yet
never be old followed by sudden flittings off
returnings dippings circlings wings winging
downward now up up against the ultraviolet
another star close enough to cup in the palms
noiseless glistening in the cruel brilliance my
turbid thoughts flutter toward his luminescence
blind. utterly

flies into him/fries

DREAM 1345

i wake to the report of hard-running water. my
view of the bathroom door is framed in muted yellow
light. i shake my somnambulant lover and hiss
    someone is in the head.
he throws the covers askew and i rise to follow
his cautious moves my one arm fearfully at his shoulder
the other at his waist. i tremble in the coolness
clad only in dread and a thin lavender gown.
abruptly the bathroom door opens inward. my father
briefly frowns out at us. his face masked in gray
we step in after him and awkwardly crowd the doorway
naked and mighty my father is a young man again, buff
and sleek the way i knew him as a child. his stream
of urine is forceful and the roar of Niagara rises
from the toilet bowl. my lover smiles, unconcerned.
"it's only Pop, sweetie, taking a piss!"
"but Pop's dead!" i shriek, grabbing him around his
neck, throwing my full weight against his. we
tumble back from the door causing it to swing partly
shut. a skeletal hand appears at the base of the
door. it beckons then vanishes. my father frowns out
at us again and i go into a shout and frantically
scoot backwards clutching my unmindful lover in
my arms, shouting to regain consciousness, shouting/
into a banshee/to banish this night haint. luckily
i manage to reawaken into this present dream

alone and still shouting

DREAM 3232

globules of silver light recede
become smaller orbs by the shrieking
instant. i am hurled outward and away
my bleeding brooding dropped thru time as the
lights shift and shimmer to form clusters of
spiraling galaxies as faster i plunge
from the frame into a vat of fleshy darkness. the
ceiling clams shut overhead. walls umbrella
upward to a tomblike close. the bed shrouds me
in tulips of soul-cold bleached cotton. lightning
exalts the windows cloaked in pale slate toile
where a fierceness flies/frantic batting raven
wings. i reach to free the trapped bird/feel his
death-grip/my father's large-boned earth-colored
talons pull me into the panes which shatter
in my ears/the alarm sounding sunrise and the
second rain of storm-laden spring

DECOR (2)

word processor digital clock books galore

there's a smoke alarm fitted to the ceiling
a fat gray long-haired cat waiting to be fed
there's a drawer of outdated wills
in the event of the unexpected there are hi-tech
metal lamps that burn hotly when on. the chairs are
as wooden and as rigid as the back of the user. there
are abstract expressionist paintings that blaze as hotly
as the lamps. there are quake-cracked white walls and
shelves of tarnished dust-ridden mementos

the window is forced open. an entry is made
it is time to revise history

MASTECTOMY

the fall of
velvet plum points and umber aureolae

remember living

forget cool evening air kisses the rush of
liberation freed from the brassiere

forget the cupping of his hands the pleasure
his eyes looking down/anticipating

forget his mouth. his tongue at the nipples
his intense hungry nursing

forget sensations which begin either
on the right or the left. go thru the body
linger between thighs

forget the space once grasped during his ecstasy

sweet sweet mama you taste so

RETURN TO DJERASSI

up skyline off bear gulch & solitude
tao receives. tao and the red-tailed hawk

here rivers of grass the welcome shade of
redwoods. deer. a riderless swing
here art defines residence
for the wounded womb-weary explorers of interiors

here. a gift from the woman poet. perhaps she
couldn't tolerate such beauteous pain. perhaps
that day she rode out on a thunderhead
never looking back. perhaps

below this latitude alice serves staunch coffee,
eggs-over-easy and short stacks to
black-and-red leather-clad ninja bikers who zoom in
ritualistically fleeing the corporate swamps of
San Francisco eager to exchange smokes or memories of
the Summer of Love

above, blue eden
where words bloom after brisk cool rains of thought

here

the only time that exists
is the time i create

265

JAZZ WAZZ

my heart in my ear his baby we need to talk jazz
later as in after the rain sleeping in the ghost
of his arms the essence of a beard tickling the roots
of wag about jobs not gotten and the life i'd live if
only you'd get with it jazz couldn't fill enough hours
trying to avoid the phone which did not ring the letter that
didn't arrive the love that was not stolen in sufficient
quantities. oh i said and oh the mirror answers
each time we pretend you are never on my mind

SWEET MAMA WANDA TELLS FORTUNES
FOR A PRICE (4)

outside the door
echo footfalls
his exit
the voyeur

vision/a lover
not yet a lover
of flesh
flesh no more

the hour
unrecorded by the clock

the stink
satisfaction
fills the room

in his arms
i smile
surrounded by lavender roses
burning candles
the music of joyous sleep
the cool veil of night

hungry no more

STRAYHORN

my ears extract his actuality from an essence
decades done

daydreams

the jaunty juxtaposition of lush notes
first takes my mind then delivers it

silver and slithery pleasures

(billy
piano piano piano me again)

later he climbs into bed the cold of his body
against my warmth evokes

strings and the aureate sopranos of
mortal tongues gone angelic — an invocation of
lounge lizards and dance floor dons

betuxed bedazzled and bathed in bubbly

and yet you speak so eloquently as you
address my guns-and-butter pain. all i do is
listen again listen again

thinning grooves

embraced by a time never mine
to live. embraced and revived

SOUL EYES

— after Coltrane

like twin hearts beating in amber
(flesh) the smoke of a caress rising and
risings/like soaring his entering my secret
solitude where night fighters prowl the terrain
like oboes tickling my ears drawing me into
reverie the lingering tingle of his stubble to
my cheek loving the mist reminiscent of his
recent evaporation like cool desert sand sifting
thru my toes his skin again taunting/begs
me for enfoldment/seducing me into amnesia
like hands softly rhythming on gone congas
summoning groin pulsations/lifting me
by invisible tongues beyond fear latitudes

like sent like received

WHAT MUST BE REMEMBERED

something i have forgotten
perhaps. once. maybe.

the way the door closed with a thin echo
describing the cheapness of the room's rental

the way the mirror distorted all it saw
elongated faces and fears

the toilet its scoured thin white
plastic mouth which squeaked
under pressure

the coffee maker stained with
years of spilt java

the furtive moves of light stealing
in past drawn window shades
denying the soulful dark

the quick brush of hurried lips and
breath the too-sweet buss of mint

the confession of bodies
to the urge

NOCTURNE

running in place
my tongue has grown strong and hard

my pace is steadier my step surer
measured as circles move around me and define
this frayed self the center of at least one stubborn
cosmos

here i sweat the days
humming because rhythm makes persistence possible
occasionally breaking into song-and-dance

aware of the weight that impedes momentum
aware of wind factor and traction

(to wish i were dead? easy. the one wish that
always comes true)

as the hum of unseen fellow runners
urges me on thru this brilliant fruitless flight

point of departure is a certainty
arrival a myth

as i streak along the beginning turning back on
itself again and again. my focus dead ahead

peering. to see if
this is the dark that precedes dawn

or the darkness before the dark

Printed March 1993 in Santa Barbara & Ann
Arbor for the Black Sparrow Press by Mackintosh
Typography & Edwards Brothers Inc. Text set in
Baskerville by Words Worth. Design by Barbara Martin.
This edition is published in paper wrappers;
there are 250 hardcover trade copies;
125 hardcover copies have been numbered & signed
by the author; & 26 copies handbound in boards
by Earle Gray are lettered & signed by the author.

Photograph: Leigh Wiener

Everytime her hands take flight her heart rides with them. It takes maximum effort to unshroud her mind's eye from the raucous inner theatre of her feelings and set her hands in motion/ do that poetic waltz, heady-handed, floating above the world as she creates and recreates it/her universe imagined and revealed/depths hidden—a reality once loved once lived. The doing is manifest as her poems, short stories and essays continue to appear. A recording artist as well, her most recent solo release is *Berserk on Hollywood Blvd.* (New Alliance). She co-hosts "The Poetry Connexion," an interview program with Austin Straus for Southern California's Pacifica radio station. *Hand Dance* is the sixth book by this Los Angeles poet and short story writer.